ONE HUNDRED LIFETIMES

AN ASPEN COVE SMALL TOWN ROMANCE

KELLY COLLINS

BOOK NOOK PRESS

CHAPTER ONE

Poppy Dawson walked into Sheriff Aiden Cooper's office with one thing on her mind. If she couldn't get Mark Bancroft to marry her, she'd have to murder him. The problem with her plan was if Mark Bancroft got anywhere near her outside of work, her father would do the job first.

She took a seat at the corner desk and pulled her notebook from the drawer to jot down reason number 132 for why she loved him. It was the same reason as the other 131 before it. At twenty-eight, she'd never loved anyone else. Since that day on the playground twenty-one years ago when he stopped Brian Decker from pulling her pigtails, it had always been Mark.

Her most memorable moment with the man of her dreams happened just over four months ago when she pinned him against the wall and stole the kiss she'd wanted her whole life.

It was an amazing kiss that lasted at least four seconds. That was when Sheriff Cooper walked into the office, caught them, and said her father was looking for her. That was the last time Mark Bancroft's lips touched hers.

She laughed. She didn't have to kill him herself, all she had to do was tell her dad he kissed her and that would be the end. In truth, she didn't want Mark in a grave. She wanted him in her bed. Pretending that she hated him was easier than knowing she loved him.

"Hey, Poppy," Sheriff Cooper said as he entered.

"New haircut?" It wasn't that she noticed the cut as much as she noticed the smell of the shampoo. The Coopers all smelled like coconut unless Aiden got a trim at Cove Cuts and then he smelled like citrus.

"Can't be looking like a vagrant." He took off his hat and set it on the filing cabinet. "Anything hot that I need to know about?"

"Wes called to ask if you could help with the wedding setup. He's got tables and chairs that need unloading." Poppy's groan happened without thought. Some girls were always a bridesmaid and never a bride. Poppy had never been either.

"He wants my help now?" he asked. "Sage and Cannon aren't getting married until the fourteenth."

"It's the twelfth," she reminded him.

"No kidding." He shuffled through a stack of papers on his desk that was two-inches high. With growth came funding, and Sheriff Cooper was filing for everything he could get, from a second deputy to new cars. "I guess I was preoccupied."

She'd like to believe it was all work, but the sheriff had been married for about four months. He'd been busy with his wife, Marina, and his adopted daughter, Kellyn. So busy that Marina was already two months pregnant. It seemed that as Louise had been pushing her eighth kid out around Christmas, Aiden had been putting one inside his wife. Some girls had all the luck.

"He said he could use a hand or two." Poppy picked up her Nikon from her desk. "I've already got a job. I'm the official photographer." She'd always loved photography but couldn't pursue it as a career. She was lucky to have a part-time job at the sheriff's office. If it weren't for her mother's ALS and expensive medications, she'd be stuck at the ranch day in and day out. She let out a sigh that could probably be heard in Kansas.

"You okay?"

She perked up. "Sure, I'm great." She stood and took a place in front of her desk. "How about a new photo for the wall? We should have one of you and Mark. You know, the sheriff and his deputy." She pointed to his desk where he took a seat and folded his hands on top.

"Like this?" He sat up tall and gave her an almost smile, trying to look serious.

After a peek into the camera she knew it was all wrong. While he looked professional, the pile of papers on his desk didn't. She set the camera down and went about setting the stage. Everything looked different from behind the lens.

When she was certain she had it right, she took the shot. "You should give them a hand. I'll lock up when I leave."

"Thanks, Poppy," He pocketed his keys and walked toward the door. "How are your sisters doing?"

She smiled at the thought of Rose, Lily, and Daisy. "They're great. I'm so proud of them." If it wasn't for her staying behind and caring for their mom, her sisters would have never been allowed to go off to college, but Lloyd Dawson couldn't argue when they all received scholarships. Rose was close by at Colorado State, studying agriculture. Lily had ventured further west to Arizona State to study engineering, while Daisy was in South Dakota diving into environmental sciences. She had her heart set on the forestry service. That left Poppy, her brother Basil and her sister Violet to pick up the pieces.

"That's great news." He plopped his hat on his head. "Your mom hanging in there?"

"Super, she's having a really good day today." She tabled her camera and went back to putting the sheriff's desk in order.

"Good to hear. Let us know if there's anything you need."

"Will do."

Sheriff Cooper left the office and Poppy to her thoughts. Those thoughts always went back to Deputy Mark Bancroft. She plopped into her seat and scrolled through the forty or fifty pictures she'd taken last week. Seventy percent of them were of him.

The door opened and in walked Sage, the bride to be. "Just the girl I'm looking for." Poppy loved Sage, who reminded her of a female Lucky Charms leprechaun or a wood sprite. She was always happy and always moving.

"What do you need?"

Sage rounded the desk. "It's not what I need but what you're going to get." She took an envelope from her purse and put it into Poppy's hand. "For your photography services."

Poppy shook her head. "That's not how it works in this town."

Sage laughed. "I know how it works. I've got a bed and breakfast, a job as Doc's nurse, and a man who's going to be waiting at the end of the aisle for me. I'm a lucky girl. I'm just spreading the love." She hopped onto the corner of Poppy's desk. "Maybe your family has forgotten how things work. We take care of our own. If you don't want it for yourself, then put it in your mother's medication fund."

A tear slipped from Poppy's eye. She opened the envelope to find several hundred-dollar bills inside. "It's too much." She pressed it toward Sage.

"It's not enough. Anyone else would charge us a fortune."

"I don't want to charge you at all."

"Take it. Don't forget I once had a mother. I wished I could have done something...anything...to keep her. I imagine your family is the same. Use it how you see fit. Give your mom a hug for me."

"I will. I know she would have loved to come to your wedding, but it's not good to tire her out."

"We understand. You can take cake and flowers home to her."

"She'd like that." Poppy tucked the envelope inside her desk drawer. Given her father's distrust of people's motives and kindness, he'd never let her accept the gift so it was a good thing she was working for it.

"Are you bringing a date?"

Poppy didn't miss the slide of Sage's eyes to Mark's empty desk.

"No, I'm not attending as a guest. This is a job."

Sage hopped off the desk. "There's plenty of time for play too. Maybe you should ask Mark." She lifted her brow.

Poppy curled her nose like she smelled something foul. "No way. He's not my type." She hated the lie that rolled so easily from her mouth.

"Really? I always thought you liked him."

Her memory went back to that kiss, then fast-forwarded to an hour later when her father found her at home and told her that he'd settled the Mark Bancroft issue once and for all. Poppy had been certain he'd shot the poor man until she showed up to work and found him at his desk. Everything had changed since that day. While he was kind and considerate, he treated her no more or no less than an employee.

"No, Mark and I are..." She shook her head. "It would never work out."

Sage gave her a look that said *I don't believe you,* but she didn't press. "Anything is possible if you want it bad enough."

"That's true, Cannon did get you to the altar on Valentine's Day."

Sage nearly skipped to the door. "Not yet, but he's got a high likelihood of success." She giggled as she walked out. Before the door shut, Sage popped her head back inside. "You know, the best way to make a man want you is to show interest in another. Luke Mosier will be at the wedding and he doesn't have a date. Should I sit you next to him?"

Poppy smiled. Luke Mosier was beyond handsome. As one of the newest residents and Aspen Cove's fire chief, he had all the girls drooling. All except Poppy because she was foolishly in love with a man she could never have.

Was anything really possible? She'd have to move mountains to get her father to accept Mark. Before that could happen, she'd have to get Mark to prove he was a better man than his father. Lloyd Dawson had a strong belief that the apple never fell far from the tree. After Mark's father, the previous foreman for the Dawsons' ranch, stole everything her dad had worked so hard to earn, he never let another stranger work his land. That's how at twenty-eight, Poppy Dawson was stuck living with her parent's and chasing a dream that never belonged to her.

Add to that her mother's debilitating disease, and she'd be lucky if she ever got a date, let alone a husband. Maybe Sage was right. Maybe it wasn't Poppy who had to prove herself to anyone. Wasn't it time Mark showed her father he was the man she knew him to be? She shouldn't have to fight for his place in her life. He should be fighting for her place in his.

She straightened her spine. "You know what? I'd love to sit next to Luke. Please, if it's not too much trouble, could you place Mark close enough to see me, but too far to engage?"

Sage let out a hoot that could be heard down the street. "You got it. This is going to be fun."

Poppy packed up her desk and set the phones to transfer to Mark's cell. "Yes, as long as no one gets shot." She put the envelope into her purse and took her jacket from the coat rack in the corner.

"You taking off early?"

Poppy walked to the door. "Yes. If I'm going to catch a fireman, I have to turn up the sizzle."

The women walked out the door and Poppy locked up. "Do you really want to catch a fireman?"

"Of course not, but Mark doesn't know that."

Sage gave her a hug. "I knew you had it in you!"

They walked side by side until Poppy reached her pickup truck, a beat-up old thing that used to belong to the ranch. The door creaked open, and she tossed her purse on the seat.

"The question is, does Mark have it in him? The bigger question is will he take the bait?"

"Something tells me he might."

It took Poppy several pumps to the gas pedal and two turns of the key for the engine to cough to life. She drove out of town toward home. Never in a hundred lifetimes would she think she and Mark could be possible, but Sage said it herself. Anything was possible if you wanted it bad enough. There were several things she wanted in this life.

One was for her mother to get healthy. Given her diagnosis of ALS, that would never happen. Two was to be able to pursue her dream of photography. Now that the Guild Creative Center was a reality, she still had a whisper of a dream that she'd one day have a studio there—a place where she could show off her photographs. The last but most important thing she truly wanted was Mark. Everything seemed like a pie-in-the-sky dream, but hey, a girl could dream.

CHAPTER TWO

Mark had two suits to his name—one for funerals, and one for weddings. He put on the light gray suit and paired it with a crimson tie. He didn't like the grim look staring back at him in the mirror. Weddings should be happy affairs, but he hadn't much cared for them lately. One consolation was his gray suit had been used far more than the navy blue, which was a good thing.

Aspen Cove was becoming a regular lover's paradise. As people came to town, they found their soul mates, and one by one all his friends were getting married. Cannon Bishop was the last of the originals—the locals he'd grown up with who he swore they would die bachelors. Today Cannon was marrying Sage. The matrimony madness started with Katie and Bowie, then it was Ben and Maisey, Aiden and Marina, and Charlie and Trig. Dalton was engaged to Samantha, no doubt ready to get hitched. Hell, even Doc had Agatha. Mark had no one. All he had was the memory of a much too short kiss with the woman he'd been obsessed with for so long he couldn't remember a time he didn't love her.

Maybe he should wear his funeral suit. With each

wedding, a piece of him died. A dream of a wife and children crushed.

He tugged the tie to his neck and straightened the knot. He ran his fingers through his hair and spritzed on the cologne Poppy always commented on when he wore it. He found himself wearing it all the time just so he could catch her inhaling deeply. He loved the way her eyes closed and her features softened like she smelled freshly baked bread. Poppy Dawson was the woman for him. It sucked that he couldn't have her.

The bottle of cologne went back to its place right next to the cheap stuff he used when Poppy wasn't around.

He liked things tidy and neat. He actually hated clutter. He chuckled, thinking about Poppy and how she spent the first ten minutes of her day straightening his desk. He made it a point to keep things in disarray so she'd feel compelled to clean it up. He wondered if she truly hated the clutter or if helping him somehow brought her what it brought him—a chance to connect.

He loved the way she brushed past him to get to the other side. The way her fingers skirted over his shoulders as she moved behind him. The way her breasts touched his back when she reached for the stacks of papers that would be easier to pick up from the front. It was pure pleasure and terrible torture at the same time.

He pocketed his keys and walked down the hallway to the living room. Poppy would have a heart attack if she saw his place. Not that it was messy, but it was in disarray as he had started on the final refurbishing project. All the walls were gone. What was once a living room, dining area, and kitchen was now one large room.

It made sense to have a great room—a space where the family could interact together. When he'd lived in the house as a child, his mother stayed in the kitchen while his father lived in a La-Z-Boy chair in the corner of the living room. Once his old man deserted them, the chair was the first thing his mother tossed to the curb. She said she had a hard time telling one from the other.

That was twenty years ago and Mark hadn't seen his father since, but he felt his presence every damn day.

Why? He'd been asking that question for two decades. Why did he have to steal the Dawsons' life savings? In doing so, he stole everything from Mark.

With thoughts of his father came thoughts of his mother. She'd moved to Pennsylvania once Mark got his job as the deputy sheriff. She signed over the house and went to live with her sister.

He picked up his phone and gave her a ring.

"Hey, sweetie," his mother answered. "You off today?"

"Not really, I'm never actually off. I may not be in the office or patrolling the streets, but I'm on call." He tugged at his tie to loosen it a tad. "What about you? How's your weekend?"

"You know me, I was up early and at the farmer's market."

Mark loved how his mother always found her niche. She was never one to let the world run roughshod over her. "How'd you do?"

"Came back empty-handed. Sold every last jar."

His mother had taken up jam making when she got to her sister's house. He missed her preserves. No one in town could make raspberry jam like his mom. No one but Poppy, but since her mother's health had taken a turn for the worse, he hadn't been gifted a jar of jam in years.

"So, are you doing okay? Do you need money?"

"If I were there, I'd pull your ear for not listening. Didn't you hear me tell you I sold all my jam jars?"

"Yes, but how much could that really be? How many did you bring?" Mark thought she'd have brought twenty or so. He opened the refrigerator and looked at his store-bought jelly as he reached for a soda.

"Aunt Theresa and I upped our production. We decided to make a real go of it. We've got local stores carrying our brand. We call it Old Gals in a Jam and today we sold one hundred and fifty jars for six bucks each."

"Holy shit." He quickly did the math. That was nine hundred dollars' worth of fruit and sugar.

"Language," she reminded him. It didn't matter that he was closing on thirty soon, she'd always be his mother. "We're doing good. The house is paid for, so all we have to do is pay taxes and die, and of course, eat those donuts from the corner shop."

Even when she lived here, she had a thing for baked goods.

Mark needed to leave if he was going to make the wedding on time. "I've got to go, Mom, Cannon is getting married today."

There was a squeal on the other end. "Tell him congratulations." She stayed silent for a breath. "What about you? I'd like some grandbabies."

He faked a laugh that sounded more like a bout of indigestion. "Got to find a girl first, Mom."

She growled. It was a sound that always came with a headshake. "You found the girl when you were nine. The problem isn't her or you. It's her father. He's got his head shoved so far up his patootie, he can't see what a great man you are."

They blew kisses into the phone before they hung up.

Mark rushed to his cruiser. It was one of the perks of the job. Being on call meant he was on duty twenty-four/seven, so there wasn't a problem using the SUV.

The drive was short, but it was filled with his last run-in with Lloyd Dawson. Poppy's father had taken him aside after Aiden's wedding—after the kiss—and told him that Poppy was off-limits. She needed a man who could provide a good life for her—a man who loved cattle and ranches as much as she did because that was how she was raised. He put his hands on Mark's shoulders and squeezed. The pressure was hard enough to bring a lesser man to his knees. He told Mark he'd never be that man.

Mark couldn't argue that fact. While he knew how to saddle and ride a horse, he knew nothing about cattle ranching. Lloyd made it clear that Poppy's life was the ranch. Was she on the same page as her father?

He parked his car in front of the Guild Creative Center and walked inside. It was a beautiful place to hold the ceremony. Being winter, the chill in the air made it impossible to use the outdoor pergola and covered pavilion. There was no need when the town had a place like this. It was over-the-top romantic with hundreds of flowers, fairy lights twinkling everywhere, and yards and yards of pink fabric.

Mark looked for Poppy in the crowd. She was hard to miss, or maybe it was simply that he was always attracted to her. He loved her smile and the way her laughter shot up an octave. Adored the way the auburn highlights in her brown hair seemed to catch fire when the sun hit it just right. There could be a million beautiful women around, but he only had eyes for Poppy.

He scanned the room and found her sitting beside Luke Mosier, Aspen Cove's new fire chief and local heartthrob. The women came from Copper Creek and Silver Springs just to get a glimpse of him. Standing, he was as tall as a building, and not much smaller seated.

The way he smiled at her filled Mark with jealousy. Poppy was Mark's, or she should be. He had to go after what he wanted. Lloyd Dawson be damned. The seat on the other side of Poppy was empty. He made his way toward it but was too late when her sister Violet slid into it before he could get there. It didn't matter anyway because Poppy stood with her camera hanging around her neck. She picked it up and looked through the lens. In the distance, the faint sound of the shutter clicked over and over.

Not wanting to sit next to Luke, he moved to the back row where Abby Garrett sat. She patted the seat next to her and smiled.

"Look at you, handsome." She tapped the knot at his necktie and smiled. "You look damn fine in a suit."

Abby was a nice woman. No doubt several years older than Mark, or at least she looked it. Then again, she spent most of her time outdoors with her bees. She was attractive and had always shown a passing interest in him, but he had eyes for another.

"How are the bees?"

She'd lost a hive during a fire at Samantha's cabin and gained another when they moved into the wall of the apartment above the bakery, which was what had forced his friends Lydia and Wes together. He mentally added them to his list of blissfully happy couples.

"They're still in hibernation, but I'm hearing some action and seeing a few of the early risers already." She craned her neck to look forward. "I didn't know Poppy was dating Luke."

Mark fought everything inside himself to look but

failed. His eyes went straight to where Poppy stood with her camera focused on Luke.

"Neither did I." This was a turn of events he neither expected nor was prepared for. The knot in his stomach twisted and turned until he was certain he'd throw up. Was he too late to get the girl of his dreams?

"They look good together."

"Poppy would look good with anyone. She shows up and raises the bar of loveliness." It was a thought he hadn't intended to vocalize.

"Still holding the torch, huh?" Abby craned her neck to get a better look at Poppy.

"No, there's nothing going on with Poppy and me."

Abby laughed so loud several people turned to see what was so funny. "How does that lie taste on your lips?"

"Like acid."

"How long are you going to wait before you make your move?"

He looked around the room at all the people in town before he brought his eyes back to Abby. She was staring at Thomas, another new firefighter who had transferred from Copper Creek.

"Tell you what, I'll make my move when you make yours on Thomas."

Abby seemed to disappear in her seat. "Oh no, that man's so far out of my league."

"Welcome to my world."

An hour later and the ceremony was over. The crowd moved into another room filled with round tables and seating assignments. As luck would have it, he was assigned to Poppy's table. He considered trading seating cards with Luke so he was next to her, but they found their seats before he could make the switch.

"Mark," Poppy said as she approached. "Do you know Luke?"

Mark eyed the man in front of him. He knew him. Knew that he was a good man and the kind of guy Lloyd Dawson wanted his daughter to marry.

"Yes." Mark held out his hand to shake. "How's it going?"

"Couldn't ask for a better life. Job is great. The town is better." Luke pointed to Poppy. "Spending time with a gorgeous girl on a Saturday afternoon is perfect."

Mark wished he had a clever remark, but he didn't. "Poppy is the prettiest girl in town." Those were the truest words.

"Pretty and smart and a rancher. Girl after my own heart."

Pink rushed to Poppy's cheeks at his words.

Mark fisted his hands. His instincts were to push the man out of the way so he could move into the vacated spot, but that wasn't him. It was better to point out the man's weaknesses politely. Put them on even footing with a simple question.

"You know about ranching?" He held his breath and waited for his reply. Knowing Luke was originally from Denver, he hoped he was a city slicker through and through.

"Oh yeah, I grew up on M and M Ranch outside of Denver. Mike Mercer and his daughter Mickey owned it. Lived in cabin six until I was eighteen and decided I wanted to fight fires. My old man left the ranch when the owner died, but I can brand cattle and rope a steer as well as the next guy."

Mark felt his world crack and crumble before him. The damn man was perfect for Poppy. How could he compete?

CHAPTER THREE

The look of defeat on Mark's face broke Poppy's heart. It was her intent to make him jealous, not give up.

She lifted her camera. "Smile." Through the lens, she saw him clearly. Over the years, she'd watched him change from a gangly teen to the man she saw today. He was handsome in a raw masculine kind of way with his three-day scruff carefully trimmed. His hair brushed back to reveal eyes that could melt her soul. Looking into those eyes through the lens of her camera, she saw a mix of emotions race through him. Hurt to jealousy to resignation. Just as she was about to ask him to step aside and talk to her, Bowie Bishop tapped the microphone and gave a toast to his brother Cannon and his wife Sage.

Poppy went back to work, snapping notable pictures. There were so many memories to capture. At *her* wedding, she'd want a picture of the toast, the cake cutting, and the first dance. Every person who shared that beautiful day with her would be memorialized in a big photo album.

When she closed her eyes and imagined her wedding day and her groom, she saw Mark. Sage was right, it was time to go after what she wanted, but when she turned around, Mark's seat was empty. A glance around the room came up empty. He was gone.

POPPY WOKE UP EARLY, exhausted from getting little sleep. Her mother, Carol, had a rough go of it last night and Poppy stayed up making sure she was okay. She could have woken her brother Basil or her sister Violet, but they had cattle to move and needed their rest. Poppy had been Carol's main caregiver for years now. She bathed her mother, fed her, changed her, and put her to bed. She did all the things a fifty-two-year-old woman should have been able to do for herself but couldn't.

ALS was an awful disease that snuffed out a life too quickly. No one had noticed anything amiss with her mom until she was basically dragging her right foot. Carol had spent all of her time on the back of a horse and muscle fatigue was common after hours in the saddle.

How was a family supposed to cope with a disease that had no known cure? How were they supposed to care for a woman who had spent her entire life caring for others? They plugged along, that's how. If Poppy had to stay up for twenty-four hours to make sure her mother was still breathing in the morning, she did it.

Last night she'd returned from the wedding late. Her father was already in bed, but her mother had been up, sitting in her wheelchair in front of the television. She hadn't been able to clear the phlegm from her throat. Her breaths had been slurpy, sounding like she inhaled fluid instead of air. After a round of breathing treatments, Carol had fallen asleep with a small rattling sound in her chest.

Poppy checked on her mother this morning before she raced to the shower. Lloyd helped with Carol in the mornings, and she was in her usual place, sitting in front of the television.

It was part of their routine to have coffee together and her mother was intent on living her life as normally as she could.

Dressed in jeans and a flannel shirt, Poppy sat down with her mom for their morning ritual. She knew these moments were coming to an end. The disease had already stolen so much. Carol couldn't walk. Hell, she had a hard time breathing when seated. Her muscles were shot, so outside of sitting in a chair or lying in bed all day, there wasn't much she could do. Thankfully, she could still speak. There was no doubt in Poppy's mind she'd lose that ability soon. Once diagnosed with ALS, most patients died within two years. Carol was going on over three. While Poppy would like to believe it was the care she gave her mom that kept her here, she knew it was her mom's will and determination to live.

"Tell me more about the wedding?" Her head bobbed forward.

Poppy adjusted the headrest of her mother's wheelchair and lifted a fresh cup of coffee to her lips. She took the tiniest of sips and choked. Soon her ability to swallow would be gone and they'd be living with feeding tubes and the need for a full-time nurse.

Warmth heated her insides as she described the day in detail from the three-tier cake Katie had made to the tulle garland. "It was so over-the-top romantic but it was perfect."

"Did you dance?" Her mother's blue eyes sparkled in the early morning light.

Poppy had wanted to dance. In her fantasy world,

Mark would have approached her and Luke on the dance floor and tapped his shoulder, asking to step in like it happened in the movies. Luke would have stepped aside while she fell into Mark's arms. She would have waltzed with him around the room to the open door where they could escape for a quiet moment. But that only happened in Hollywood. There were no dances. No open doors to an abandoned patio. No Mark because he left before the dancing began.

"No, although Luke Mosier, the fire chief, asked me to dance once."

"Luke?" Mom's eyes grew wide. There would have been a lift to her brow if her muscles had allowed it. "What about Mark?" she whispered.

What about Mark? Poppy rubbed her eyes. "He left early." She debated telling her mother the whole plot to her jealousy plan. It wasn't much of a risk to tell her mother, she'd never have the energy to repeat the tale. From the beginning, she'd told Poppy that a heart didn't get to choose who it loved. Her father would disagree.

Her mom lifted her hand. It took every bit of energy for her to push her palm forward to set it on top of Poppy's. "You love who you love."

If only it was that easy. "But Dad hates Mark."

Carol cleared her throat. "He hates the idea of Mark. How can you hate a man you don't know?" Her hand flopped down to hang next to the chair. "Your father is stubborn as a goat. Behind the tough exterior is a soft man afraid of losing everything he's got." A tear ran down her cheek. "I don't have long. He knows that, and it scares the living daylights out of him. He's not one for change."

She considered the words her mother spoke. Was her father truly afraid? Did he keep an iron fist on the family because that was the only thing he thought he could control? It was all too much to consider.

"You can't leave us." Poppy held back the tears that wanted to gush. Once they started, she might never stop crying. "I need you."

A soft smile lifted her mother's lips. It was a rare thing to see these days. "I will leave you and you will go on but you have to stand up for yourself." Her eyes moved to the camera on the table. "Chase your dreams, not your fathers."

Poppy pulled her chair next to her mom's. She picked up the camera and started clicking through the images. When she came to the picture of Mark, her mom said, "He looks as miserable as you."

"Yes, he does." She kissed her mother's cheek and stood. There were chores to do and a life to live. Her life. "You want to watch TV or lay down?"

Her mom's lids were heavy. "I think I'll sleep."

Poppy helped her mother into bed and kissed her. She'd check on her after her chores.

While she collected eggs and cleaned the stalls of their horses, she planned. Today was the first day of her life. While she respected her father, she also had to respect herself.

Watching her mother deteriorate so quickly made it painfully obvious that life was short. When she got back to the house, she showered again and dressed for work at the sheriff's office.

Every day she prepared a meal before she left. Without realizing it, she'd taken her mother's place. While she loved her siblings, they weren't the family she craved. She couldn't be everyone's everything. Not when she only wanted to be Mark's something.

She moved her mother to her favorite chair and gave her

a kiss before she walked to the door. "I love you," she said because each day she left might be the last she'd be able to say those words to her mom.

As she reached for the doorknob, it opened. Her father kicked off his boots and walked inside.

"Where are you off to?" He frowned at her dress.

"I work today at the sheriff's office."

He narrowed his eyes. His bushy brows almost met in the center of his forehead. "It's Sunday," he grumbled.

"Yes, it is. Have you ever known the sheriff's office to close?"

"Who are you working with today?"

Poppy knew what he was really asking.

"Dad, I love you, but you have to get over it. I work with Mark. My job pays for Mom's meds." She looked at her mom, who had managed to lift half her mouth into a smile.

Her father gave her the trifecta of disappointment, which included a shake of his head, a frown, and a growl. "I don't like it."

Poppy glanced at her mother, who looked like she was laughing inside.

"You don't have to like it, but you have to deal with it." She lifted on tiptoes and kissed his cheek. "Lunch is in the refrigerator. Mom will need her meds at noon." She stepped through the door.

"Have a good day," he said.

His words almost stopped her, but she kept moving. In fact, she had some pep in her step that she hadn't felt for years.

"You too, Dad. I'll see you later." Poppy winked at her mother before she closed the door and headed to the old truck.

She climbed inside and pumped the gas several times

before she twisted the key. This time the old girl started on the first try. Things were looking up, after all.

She'd started the process of standing her ground with her father today. The results were positive. One stubborn man down, and another to go. When she got to work, Mark Bancroft was in for a surprise. Yesterday he might have looked defeated, but that's because he didn't remember what he was fighting for. Her plan was to walk inside and steal another kiss—a kiss that he wasn't likely to forget.

CHAPTER FOUR

The office smelled of her perfume like somehow her scent had soaked into the drywall to torture him. Having Poppy around was like being on a diet. She was a damn glazed donut, hot from the oven, and he couldn't have her.

He walked into the empty space and took his seat behind his desk, which was neat as a pin thanks to Poppy. Normally, there would be a note tacked in the center. It always had a kind word or a positive affirmation on it but today his desk was empty, so he opened his drawer and reached into the very back where he'd tucked every note she'd ever given him.

After thumbing through the pile, he pulled out his favorite. The one that said she missed him when he spent the day in Copper Creek for training. He placed it in the center of his desk pretending she'd left it yesterday.

He leaned back in his chair and stared at the yellow sticky note. While the wedding had been great, seeing Poppy with Luke was like getting shanked by a dull rusty blade. It was important to look at things for what they were. His mother always told him to be honest with himself. The truth was painful. When comparing Luke Mosier to himself, it was like comparing apples to watermelons. There was no comparison.

Luke had him by at least four inches and thirty pounds. That wasn't where the differences ended. He was the fire chief whereas Mark was a deputy. He drove a fancy high-end SUV while Mark had the cruiser along with the motorcycle stored in his garage. Luke was a cowboy at heart, something Lloyd would value in a man. Most importantly, Luke's father hadn't robbed the Dawsons, leaving them destitute for years.

It was a wonder that Poppy didn't hate him too. How many new dresses had she had to forfeit so her family could eat. As a child Mark couldn't begin to imagine what his father's betrayal cost the family. He only knew what it cost him and that was his access to the Dawsons, who were like his own family.

There were no more barbecues. No more horseback rides. Nothing but dirty stares and ugly comments. He picked up the note from his desk and tucked it back into his drawer. "I miss you too."

Rather than dwell on what he couldn't have, he opened the file on his desk and filled out the forms for things that were possible like upgraded equipment. Aiden had taken care of the bigger items like cars and weapons and left the smaller equipment like office supplies to him.

The old computer on Poppy's desk had been around for at least a decade. It was a surprise it actually functioned, but somehow Poppy always made things work. She was a survivor. Hell, she put up with her cantankerous father. At twenty-eight she lived at home to care for her mother. He knew she'd given up her chance to go to college so her sisters could. She'd been the Dawsons' sacrificial lamb for far too long. Wasn't it time she got something good?

After scrolling down the list, he found her a state-of-the-art system. It would take up most of the office budget, but it was important for her to have what she needed. He ticked off the box and moved on to mundane supplies like paper and pens.

At exactly nine o'clock the door opened and in walked Poppy smelling like cinnamon, sugar, and sin.

"Good morning."

Her smile made his heart race.

"That must have been some wedding reception." He took her in from her broad smile to the skip in her step as she rushed in with a box of muffins.

"You should have stuck around. It was such a great night." She tucked her purse into her drawer and headed for the coffeepot. "You want coffee?"

He wanted to smack himself upside the head. He should have made the coffee, but he was too busy lamenting the reasons he couldn't make her happy when in truth, a fresh pot of coffee would have been a good start.

"You sit down. I'll make the coffee."

Her perfect little brows rose. "You're making the coffee?" She set the muffins on the table and pressed her hand to his forehead. "You don't feel like you have a fever."

"I'm capable of making coffee."

She opened the box of banana nut muffins and arranged them on a pretty dish she'd brought from home when she started working here.

"I know you're capable. Why now, when you haven't made a pot of coffee in months?"

He cringed inside. He wasn't all that different from his

father, after all. He'd taken from Poppy without giving anything in return.

"Because I haven't made a pot of coffee in months. I'm sorry for that. I should have been helping you all along." He took the pot to the sink in the back and filled it up with water. When he got back, she was at her desk waiting for the dinosaur of a computer to start up.

Once he had it brewing, he went back to his space and continued to order supplies.

"I'm getting you a new computer." He held out the catalog to her. "Is there anything else you need?"

She took it and looked through what he'd marked for order.

He hated it when she frowned. The way she twisted her lips made him want to kiss them back into a smile, but that wasn't his job. As of yesterday, her kisses belonged to Luke. The thought of it made his stomach clench.

She pointed to the coffeepot and the catalog. "Why all this now?"

He could tell her a thousand reasons why she deserved better but all he said was, "We got extra funding and you have the oldest equipment. It's a simple upgrade."

She nodded. "Thank you." She pressed her finger to the order form and worked her way down the list. "Do you mind if I adjust some of these numbers? We'll need more pens if you and Sheriff Cooper keep losing them. We also need more Post-it Notes." She looked at his desk and shook her head.

"Sure, get whatever you need." He hated that his voice was tinged with resignation. Up until Cannon and Sage's wedding, he'd at least been able to fantasize about a future with her. Seeing her with Luke made the fantasy disappear.

She cocked her head to the side. "Are you okay?"

"Yes. Just tired."

"I should be after spending hours on my feet, but I feel good."

He grabbed his keys and stood. "Danced all night, huh?"

She laughed. "I danced some, but mostly I took pictures." She opened her drawer and pulled her Nikon from her bag. "You want to see?"

"Maybe later. I have to do my rounds."

Her face fell as she tucked her camera back inside the drawer. "Okay, I'm here until noon today."

He grabbed a muffin from the table. "Thanks for picking these up."

She shrugged. "Not a big deal. They always have a box waiting for you guys and the fire station."

Had she delivered theirs too?

"Thanks for taking care of us." He hated to ask, but he needed to know. "Did you deliver a box to the fire station?"

She approached the table and picked up her muffin, pulling the top free. "I don't work for them. They can get their own free muffins." She took a bite of the crown and hummed. "So good."

The sounds she made caused a twitch in his pants. "Thanks for getting ours."

She swallowed and smiled. "I know how much you like your muffins. I aim to please."

The way she emphasized the word *your* made his heart feel full.

"I'll try to be back before you leave for the day."

She licked her lips and he couldn't take his eyes off the slick sheen she left behind.

"That would be great because I have something to give you."

"Really? What?"

She moved toward him. With her hand at his back, she guided him to the doorway. "It's a surprise. So, hurry back."

He walked out the door but watched her return to her desk through the window. The sway to her hips made him embarrassingly hard. Then there were her legs. Damn long legs that he'd wrapped around his waist thousands of times in his dreams. He looked at his hardening length. He needed to get away before he had to arrest himself for indecent exposure.

When he turned from the window, he found Doc Parker setting up a ladder in front of his little drugstore and clinic across the street.

Nothing shrank a boner faster than worry. Watching Doc climb onto the ladder sent Mark into a panic.

"Doc, you shouldn't be on a ladder at your age." Mark rushed to where Doc splashed soapy water on the window.

"I'm old, not dead, son." He sponged the cleaner across the glass.

"You might be both if you slip and fall."

Doc's girlfriend Agatha Guild, joined them. "Get down from there, you old coot. I just got you in my life. I won't lose you to something as silly as a tumble."

Doc grumbled, "They aren't going to clean themselves, lovey."

Even Doc Parker was in love and getting more kisses and action than Mark. That thought made sure the twitch in Marks pants was gone.

Mark reached up and took the sponge from Doc. "Get down from there. I'll clean them."

"Shouldn't you be doing something else?" Doc asked as he stepped from the last rung to the sidewalk.

"My job is to serve and protect. Cleaning your windows

does both. I'm performing a service and protecting both of us from Agatha's wrath if you had taken a fall."

Doc wrapped his arm around her and kissed her cheek. "Love does crazy things to you."

"I wouldn't know." Mark swiped the soaked sponge across the glass and watched the water cascade down. He pulled the squeegee from the bucket and went to work.

"Now listen here, son. You're either blind or stupid." Doc pointed to the sheriff's station. "That girl has been in love with you forever."

If only that were true. "Poppy's moved on. She's seeing Luke Mosier." Saying it out loud sent a jolt of unpleasantness to his heart.

Agatha and Doc shook their heads and *pffted* at the same time. "So, you are stupid," Doc said.

"And blind," added Agatha.

"Isn't it time you pulled your head from your keister? She won't wait forever."

CHAPTER FIVE

Poppy watched Mark from the window. She loved how he stepped in to help Doc. Loved the way he took care of everyone around him. Despite the distance he'd put between them the past few months, he'd still taken care of her. One day he'd noticed her windshield wipers were falling apart, and the next day he changed them.

Last month she'd come down with a cold, and when she got to work, she found a bag of remedies on her desk. He'd purchased everything from cough syrup to echinacea tea. Mark was a good man. Too bad she couldn't get her father to acknowledge that fact.

She spent the morning pouring over the supply catalog. It warmed her heart that Mark had allocated most of the budget to buy her a new computer. It was especially kind when his own equipment needed upgrading. His poor chair no longer adjusted. A day didn't go by without him cracking his knees on the underside of his desk. His filing cabinet drawers fell out every time they were opened. The pencil sharpener ate half the pencil before it got to the lead.

No, this order wouldn't do. There had to be a way for it

all to work. She spent the morning reconfiguring the budget. She downgraded the computer. Anything was better than what she had now. With the extra money, she upgraded the items Mark and Aiden needed.

As the morning disappeared, she kept an eye on the front door. Each time a shadow passed the window she held her breath. Her stolen kiss plan had played out a thousand ways since he'd left. She could rush to him and tackle him like a linebacker, but that seemed too forward. Besides, that was kind of what she'd done the day of Aiden and Marina's wedding. The poor man got pushed between the wall and the coat rack. He hadn't had much of a choice but to kiss her.

This time she wanted it to be different, but she wouldn't rule out the possibility of a repeat if he tried to do the right thing, which in her mind was the wrong thing. Life was far too complicated.

Her thoughts went back to her mother. It was worrisome that her condition was worsening. Poppy was caught between a rock and a hard place. She didn't want to leave the house to work and yet she needed the work to pay for her mom's medications. It was the perfect set of contradictory conditions.

Violet, Basil, and their father checked in on Mom frequently throughout the day, but all it would take was one turn of events to change everything. There were days she hated her father for his stubbornness and days when she understood his pride.

He couldn't afford home health care and was too proud to file for Medicaid, so that left the family responsible for her mother's care.

Doc Parker and Dr. Lydia popped in weekly to check on her, which gave Poppy comfort. She felt underqualified for the task of keeping her mother alive. Why did life have to be so hard? Why couldn't it be eased with the kiss of a man she loved? Yes, as silly as it sounded, Poppy Dawson was in love with Mark Bancroft and had been her whole life. They'd shared a single kiss and since then, she knew she wanted to share her entire life with him.

When the clock hit noon, she gave up hoping he'd be coming back before she had to leave. She'd have to wait another day to feel her lips on his. She gathered her things and stopped by the bakery to get treats for her family.

Katie was behind the counter, stocking the display case. "Back for more, huh?"

Poppy leaned over to look inside the glass case. "If I can't get a man, I'll have to settle for a muffin."

"You got time for coffee?"

Poppy looked over her shoulder as if the answer was there. She should get home, but it was Sunday and Violet would be there. She never rode the range on Sundays. Instead, she bathed Mom and cooked dinner. Violet made a mean roasted chicken and vegetables.

"I could use a coffee."

Katie pointed to the table under the Wishing Wall, a bulletin board where people filled out sticky notes with their wishes, needs, and desires. She stuck a pod into the Keurig, plated up a few treats and joined Poppy at the table.

"What's this about no man? I thought you were using Luke as bait."

Did everyone know? "Sage talks too much."

"Not really, I have eyes."

"Then you know there was nothing to see." Poppy broke off a piece of a heart-shaped cookie. It was fitting. If she couldn't mend a broken heart then she should swallow it and move on.

"Maybe you need glasses." Katie rose and rushed

behind the counter to get the coffee that had just finished brewing. She was back in seconds.

"He didn't even stay for the meal."

"I know. That's what you wanted, right? You wanted him to feel something. To get jealous."

Jealousy was definitely what she was after, but she didn't expect to be abandoned. "He left, Katie. He turned around and walked out."

Katie leaned forward and put a hand on her arm. "He couldn't stand to see you with another. What did you expect him to do? Beat Luke up?"

"Yes, I kind of did."

Katie giggled. "Really?"

In truth, Poppy never expected a fistfight, but she did hope for a fight of sorts—the kind where Mark took her by the hand and led her away. A moment where they were alone, and he told her she belonged to him.

"He could have asserted himself. He could have at least pretended I mattered."

"Maybe he did. Maybe he sacrificed what he wanted to give you for what he thought best."

Poppy put her coffee down and fisted her hands. She really wanted to hit something. Instead, she let out a growl that echoed off the walls.

"When do I get to choose for myself?"

Katie nodded. "Been there. It took me running away to Aspen Cove for my parents to open their eyes. Until then, I was twenty-seven and living at home because that was what everyone expected."

Poppy nodded. "I'm still there, except I'm twenty-eight."

Katie moved her head side to side while she was thinking. "It's tougher for you because of your mom, but you have to set the boundaries with your father. Maybe invite Mark over for dinner. Let him see the man he's become."

"Did you know my father can shoot a soda can clear off its perch from several hundred feet away with his eyes closed?"

"You forgot to add his hands tied behind his back."

"There's that too."

Katie leaned back and kicked her feet up on the empty chair beside her. "What are you really afraid of?"

Poppy sat up. "What do you mean?"

"I see several possible scenarios. One being you're afraid of what your father will do. Two being you've pined after the man for years and what if you find out he's not the one for you. Three is the chase is more exciting than the catch." She pulled her feet to the floor and leaned in. "You have to choose for yourself. Your dad will always love you. He'll come to respect or at least tolerate your decisions." Katie smiled. "Once you have his first grandchild, all will be forgiven." Katie reached up and cupped her cheek very much like her mother used to before ALS stole her strength. "Your heart decides, Poppy. You're silly if you think otherwise."

The door to the bakery opened and in walked Katie's husband, Bowie. He set their daughter Sahara on her little sneakers. She was still wobbly on her feet, but she toddled straight to her mom with a giggle. Watching her friend's happiness made Poppy's heart feel full and empty at the same time. She was happy for Katie, but wanted that for herself.

Poppy had to make some life choices if she wanted a life and a family of her own. Deep in her heart, her choice was Mark. She'd gotten a taste of standing up for herself this morning. Her poor father didn't know what he was in for.

Things in the Dawson home were changing. Poppy could no longer be an extension of her father if she wanted to be herself.

She purchased a few treats for her family and walked out of the bakery and straight into Mark.

"Poppy, sorry. I didn't see you run out." His hands set on her shoulders to steady her.

She turned to look inside the bakery. Katie stood with a bright smile and a what-are-you-going-to-do look.

"Just the man I needed to see." Before she could chicken out, she moved forward with her plan. "I need to tell you something." She walked toward her truck.

"Are you okay?"

"Never better." She opened the door and put the box of treats on the seat. "I could be better if you and I figured this whole thing out. There's something between us."

"Poppy—"

She pressed a finger to his lips. "No, you need to listen to me. I've been in love with you my whole life. When I say in love, I mean the innocent love you feel when you're a teen, but I'm not a teen anymore. I'm a woman who has dreams and desires." She let the word *desires* float slowly off her tongue.

"I—"

"Shh, you'll get your turn. Right now, it's my time to tell you how I feel."

He lifted a hand and leaned against her truck, framing her on one side. "I'm listening."

He was so close she could smell his cologne and feel his breath caress the skin on her neck. Her heart raced. Her palms grew sweaty. Dots of light danced in front of her eyes. She took a big breath to avoid fainting. This was a make it or break it moment.

She reached out and steadied herself by holding onto his arms. Arms that bunched and flexed under her fingertips. His muscles were hard like stone.

"Luke and I aren't a thing."

He cocked his head. "Didn't work out?" He genuinely looked sad for her.

"No. It wasn't meant to work out. How could I date Luke when the only person I want to be with is you? How could I kiss him when the only lips I crave are yours?"

He smiled and then frowned. "But your father—"

"Isn't kissing you. I am." She cleared her throat. "Or I will be if that's what you want. We're good together. How good is yet to be seen, but I'd like to explore more."

He stepped back and gave her a longing look. "How much more?"

The way he licked his lips made her core ache. "Way more."

He smiled. "Where do you want to start?"

She moved her hands from his arms to the back of his neck.

"How about a kiss?"

He leaned in and tentatively touched her lips with his. His body shifted forward until they were chest to chest. When one hand curled around her waist and the other cupped the back of her head, she opened her mouth. Mark dipped his tongue inside to explore. He tasted of hope and longing and love. They separated long enough to catch a breath before they kissed again. Long lazy strokes of his tongue made her moan. His leg pressed between her thighs made her quiver. When he pulled away, he nipped her bottom lip.

"Enough?" There was a glint in his eyes.

Poppy drew in a deep breath. "No, but it will have to be for now. I'm late getting home."

He pressed his lips to hers. "Drive safely, Poppy. Thanks for telling me what you wanted. I guess I needed it spelled out."

She cupped his face, loving the feel of his scruff under her palm. With the sheriff having facial hair, he couldn't very well require Mark to shave. "You didn't get a chance to tell me what you wanted."

The smile on his face warmed her insides. "I want more, so much more."

CHAPTER SIX

Doc was right when he said she wouldn't wait forever. Hell, she hadn't waited at all. That kiss was perfect and long overdue. The hell with Lloyd Dawson and his grudge. Mark was not the same man as his father. He didn't cheat, steal, or lie. Somehow, he'd prove that to Lloyd.

"How about dinner on Friday?" he asked.

Flecks of amber danced like tiny sparks in her eyes. "Friday?" She looked up like her calendar was written in the clouds. "I don't know," she said. "I'll have to check with Luke?"

He stepped back. "But you said—"

Obviously, his look of confusion was humorous to Poppy. Her shoulders shook with her laughter. "I'm teasing, you silly man." She laid her hand on his chest.

Even clothed he could feel the heat of her fingertips as she traced down his buttons to his belt. The touch was intimate and sent messages from the head on his shoulders to the one in his pants. A deep needy ache took over, causing his inner caveman to surface.

"You better be, because Luke is big and I'm not sure I can take him down but I'd die trying."

"You'd fight for me?"

"Isn't it about time I did?" He pressed his lips to hers once more. It was a sweet, lingering kiss that could have gone on forever but had to stop before Lloyd came looking for his daughter.

Mark had every intention of talking to him, but he'd do it on his terms.

"You better go home." He brushed her hair behind her ear so he could get a good look at her face. "You're so damn beautiful, Poppy." He loved the way the sun brightened the red highlights in her hair. The way the golden flecks of her eyes made the green in them glow like emeralds. Loved the tiny freckle on her eyelid that was shaped like a heart. Her lips, God he loved her lips and how soft they felt against his. When his tongue touched hers, it was like a sweet drug. No doubt an addiction he'd never be able to kick.

"You're right, I should go."

He helped her inside her truck. "I'll see you on Wednesday. Let's have lunch together and we can plan our date."

"It's a date before our date." She pumped the gas several times and turned the key. The truck whined and coughed before it started.

"You need a new truck."

She giggled. "I need a lot of things, but a new truck isn't at the top of my list."

"What tops your list?" He thought he knew everything about her. His knowledge was gleaned from years of watching her, longing for her to be his, but he'd never asked what she truly wanted. If he had, they wouldn't have waited so long to kiss.

"One more kiss for now."

He leaned over and gave her a kiss she wasn't likely to forget. "Can I call you tonight?"

She smiled, but he saw the worry in her eyes. "Umm, how about I call you? I don't want the phone to wake my mom up."

"Okay, that will work."

She closed the door and pulled out of the parking space.

He watched the back of the truck until it disappeared from his view.

Mark wondered if that was the truth. Maybe she didn't want her father to know they were dating. Were they dating? Did one scheduled date mean exclusivity? He hoped so because one thing he refused to be was Poppy's dark secret. That was one of the reasons he'd walked away after Aiden's wedding.

The memory of that day was still fresh in his mind. The fear he saw in her face the minute Aiden told her that her father was looking for her couldn't be forgotten. He'd suggested she go out the back door, but in his heart, he wanted her to walk out the front holding his hand.

Deep inside, he wanted Poppy to fight for him as well.

Then there was the run-in with her father, which he tried hard to forget but couldn't.

He finished his official shift and changed into street clothes before he went to Bishop's Brewhouse. He'd grown up with Cannon and Bowie. Though he was a few years younger, they'd always been the big brothers he'd never had.

"Coffee?" Cannon asked from behind the bar.

Mark looked around the empty bar. "Beer."

"Beer?" Cannon gave him a what's-wrong look. "You okay?"

It was a reasonable question since Mark rarely drank. If he did it was a beer or a glass of wine at home. He couldn't very well warn others about drinking and driving and do it himself, but a single beer wouldn't hurt.

His father had been a drinker and had shown him the evils of alcohol. One beer was fine, but any more than that turned his old man mean. There were plenty of days when Ben Bishop, Cannon's father and the previous owner of the bar, had called to have good ole Mick Bancroft picked up. Normally it was because he was stumbling drunk, but occasionally it was because he'd been in a fight. The first time Mark drove, he was just seven and his feet barely hit the pedals. He'd been with his father at the Dawsons' ranch. After a long day of branding cattle, Mick had had one too many and tossed the keys to Mark. That day had been the beginning of the end.

"You look troubled." Cannon put the frosty mug in front of him. "Spill it."

He tucked all thoughts of his father away. "Nothing to spill. Things are great."

"Things looked pretty great from my vantage point." He nodded toward the window. Cannon had a perfect view of the kisses Mark had shared with Poppy.

He reached under the counter for the jar of bar snacks and filled several small bowls, then placed them on the bar in preparation for the Sunday night crowd. Months ago, the Brewhouse would have never been open on Sunday, but with a steady flow of patrons, Cannon couldn't turn good money away.

"Yep, that was the highlight of my day. That and getting Mrs. Brown's cat down from her roof." He sipped his beer and let the frosty carbonation cool the heat still swirling around his insides. The heat caused by an amazing kiss and a hot, sexy woman.

"I think the cat goes up there to get away from her. What did she dress him in this time?"

Mrs. Brown never had any children, but she had a cat she named Tom. "A tuxedo jacket and a bow tie."

"Poor thing. I wonder if she dressed Mr. Brown, and that's what killed him. Better to die than have to wear another of her getups."

"Could be. He did have the silliest sweaters. He seemed to love them. She even buried him in one. Love will make you do crazy shit."

"Speaking of love. I see you finally made your move with Poppy?"

"She made the move. After the wedding, I thought she was with Luke."

Cannon laughed. "That was the plan. Sage's actually. Looks like it worked."

No doubt the whole town was in on "the plan." Small towns were a blessing and a curse. They knew everything. Mark wondered how long it would take for their kiss to reach Lloyd. They'd made a public display of it. The news no doubt traveled faster than her old truck.

"You need to take your wife on a honeymoon so she can stop meddling in my life." Though he complained, it was nice to have people care enough about him to want to intervene. Lord knew he hadn't been doing a good job of moving his life forward on his own.

"Dude, it took me almost two years to get her to the altar. I'm thinking it will take me another three to get her to leave town. She loves it here."

"What's not to love?" There was a time he'd thought he wanted to leave Aspen Cove but he couldn't abandon everything he'd worked for. He smiled as he sipped his beer. He was nothing like his father.

"What's next? Are you going to kidnap Poppy and take her to Vegas?"

The idea had crossed his mind at least a thousand times.

"Nope, I'm going to make her fall unequivocally in love with me, and then I'm going to win over her father. Family is important to Poppy. I have to respect that."

"I think you've got point one under control. There isn't a person within a fifty-mile radius who doesn't know Poppy Dawson's heart belongs to you. As for her father, that's going to be an uphill battle."

He shrugged. "I best put on my hiking shoes because I have a date with her on Friday and I plan to pick her up at home."

"You better plan to wear your bulletproof vest too."

Mark took a ten from his wallet and put it on the bar.

Cannon shook his head. "Beer's on me in celebration of your first kiss and all." While Cannon's expression was emotionless, Mark could see the humor in his eyes.

"Screw you. That was not my first kiss."

"The first one you consented to. Or so I'm told."

"Damn Aiden. Doesn't he have anything else to talk about?" Mark finished his beer and slid his mug forward.

"Not lately, unless you count how freaking in love he is with Marina and Kellyn."

Mark had to admit that his boss was head over heels. While Aiden had fallen hard and fast for Aspen Cove's hairdresser and her once silent daughter, and happily told everyone who'd listen, it had taken a lifetime for Mark to admit his feelings for Poppy.

"It's great, right?" He remembered when Kellyn didn't say a word. She'd been silenced by fear of her biological father. It was Aiden who'd unlocked her words and now the little sprout never shut up. "He bought Kellyn a sheriff's outfit. Little thing sits in her father's chair and bosses me around."

"But you love it." Cannon lifted the mug, asking silently if Mark wanted another.

He shook his head. He'd stick to his rule of one.

"I do love it." It was true. All Mark wanted was a big family. Sadly, he'd never had one himself. It was why he'd adopted most of the townsfolk as honorary kin.

He closed his eyes and imagined a life with Poppy. His small house would need an addition for the three or four kids he hoped to have. Little girls with brown hair and green eyes, and little boys who were an amalgamation of them both. He only hoped his girls didn't look like him. He'd never wish his looks on a female. Then again, if his daughters could grow a beard, he might not have to stand by the door with his shotgun. And right then, he understood Lloyd's protectiveness a little better. In fact, he respected it. If Poppy had been his daughter, he'd have never allowed her out of the house.

"I'm out of here." He swiped up his ten and left a five for Cannon.

"See you tomorrow," his friend called after him.

Mark hopped in his cruiser and left for home. The rest of the night he spent sanding kitchen cabinets and waiting for Poppy to call.

CHAPTER SEVEN

She'd come home feeling on top of the world only to find her father waiting. The scowl on his face could curdle milk. Certain that someone from town had called and said something about the kiss, she approached him with a half apology on her lips. That's when things went from bad to worse.

Maybe leading with "It was just a kiss. A long overdue kiss" was not the right move. When her father's face turned the color of cranberries, it was too late. Her secret was out and he was furious.

"You've been kissing that Bancroft boy? How many times do I have to tell you that he's no good? He comes from poor stock. If he were a steer, I'd have already put him down. No use passing on bad genes." He stood on the front porch with his hands on his hips. At over six feet tall, Lloyd Dawson was an opposing figure.

Standing a foot shorter, Poppy took after her mother. She was sassy but sweet, tough but tender. She'd spent her life being a good girl but that had to end. She was no longer a child. She was a woman and she had to start acting like one.

The one thing no one in the family did was question the word of her father. That was a habit that would end today.

"How old am I?" She stomped up the stairs, showing more courage than she had. When her father didn't answer, she continued. "I'm almost thirty and you treat me like I'm a damn teen."

"You're only twenty-eight." He took a step back and stared at her. "You'll always be my little girl."

Something about his words softened her stance, but that was his mode of operation. He'd run you over like an angry bull, then make you purr like a kitten with words of love and endearment.

"I can't be your little girl anymore, Dad. I'm a grown woman and I need more than you in my life." She watched his body wilt in front of her. "You can't be my everything. I need love and affection and kisses from a man who cares for me romantically."

"Poppy, I'm telling you, Mark is not your man."

She was so tired of fighting with him. Exhausted to the bone really. "You don't get to choose. My heart chose a long time ago." She thought about her mom and smiled. "Did Grandpa like you at first?"

Her father sank to the steps and pulled her down beside him. "Your grandfather respected me."

She shook her head. "You earned that over the years, but did he like you at the start?" She'd heard the stories but wondered if he'd reinvent history to make his point.

He palmed his chin and rubbed the shadow of whiskers that always seemed to bloom around noon. He was the only man she knew who could shave in the morning and be well on his way to a beard by afternoon.

"No, your grandfather didn't like me much. He thought I lacked motivation because I didn't have land or money."

"You're the most motivated man I know." Waking up at four every morning screamed motivation to her. Working every day until his bones creaked showed the world that he was driven to succeed. "Grandpa never gave you a chance because he judged you. He had made an assumption about who you were. It's the same thing you're doing to Mark."

He shifted his body to face her. "It's not the same thing at all."

"No?"

"I didn't run his ranch and steal everything from the man."

The whole conversation was ridiculous. "No, you proved to him you were worthy of his daughter and his land. You became the son he never had but always wanted."

"You're right, but I've got a son. I don't need another."

She leaned back against the porch rail. "I used to think you were so smart."

He stared at her the same way he did the day she let his prize bull loose and it took him all day to catch the beast. Pure agitation. "You're not too old to turn over my knee."

She pulled her knees to her chest and tucked her dress around her legs. "I am. And I've let you run roughshod over me for years out of respect, but you know what?" She took a deep breath because the next sentence would crush him, but it needed to be said. "I'm losing respect for you."

"Now, that's not fair. And it's no way to talk to your father." He mumbled something about this generation and disrespect.

She looked at the man who raised her. All her life she'd seen him as a reasonable man, but he wasn't. He lived by his own set of rules. Rules he made up to fit his wants and needs without consideration for others. How her mother put up with him for so long she didn't understand. How she herself allowed him to control her was another puzzle.

"You want to know what's not fair? Not fair is deciding an eight-year-old boy abandoned by his father should be punished for sins he never committed. Not fair is making me feel guilty for trying to have a life." She hated laying it all out in one go but she had to. "Don't you think I've given up enough? I stayed behind to care for Mom despite wanting to go to college."

"Family comes first." The red seeped into his skin once again. She was certain he'd implode or burst into flames.

"Don't I know it. Ten years I've been sacrificing myself for this." She spread her arms out. "The ranch, the house, the cattle."

"It's your responsibility."

She let out an unladylike growl. "No, it's not. I never asked to be a rancher. It's not what I want."

"You don't know what you want," he sniped back. He pulled the can of chew from his pocket and loaded his lower lip.

"I do know, I always have." She glanced around her at the land, the house, the cattle milling about in a far-off field. "This isn't my dream. This is yours. How many years of my life do I have to give up for you to be happy?" Her voice rose in pitch and volume until she remembered her mother was sick inside the house. "Have you ever considered what would make me happy?"

He spit into the bushes to his side. "You think I'm happy? I'm running a ranch with a skeleton crew." He turned his head to the front door and sighed. "The love of my life is inside fighting for each day of her life, and here you are telling me your life is rough. Stop being so damn selfish."

"Don't you dare," Poppy whisper-yelled so her father would know how pissed she was but her mother wouldn't hear. "That woman, the one you say is the love of your life... she's my mother, and I spend every moment I can caring for her and loving her because you're too goddamn busy running the ranch."

"You're treading on dangerous ground, young lady." His voice held a warning that she'd pushed him too far.

"Wake up, Dad, she's going to die. When she does, don't you dare tell me you wish you'd had more time with her, because guess what? You have all the time in the world. You just prefer to spend it with your cows instead."

She didn't expect the slap. It came as a surprise. Her father had never hit her before except a swat to her bottom when she'd misbehaved. Her hand came up to rub the sting from her cheek.

"Do you feel better?" she asked.

By the shock on his face, she knew he didn't.

"I'm sorry, I lost my temper." He leaned forward to touch her, but she moved out of his reach.

"At least you're responding to something." She stood and palmed the wrinkles from her dress. "Just remember that someday you'll be on your deathbed, and I'm pretty sure you won't think back and wish you'd raised more cattle. What you'll wish for is another day with Mom, a hug from one of your kids, a moment to watch the sun rise or set." Poppy stretched her hands out again. "None of this matters. You let one man's lack of integrity tarnish yours. You could have hired someone else." Her brother rode his horse toward the barn. "You said you had a son and you didn't need another." She pointed to her brother. "You have any idea what he wants? His dream isn't to raise cattle."

His eyes popped open. "What is it?" She imagined the extent of his conversations with Basil was cattle and ranch related. Basil hated the cows. He even stopped eating beef in protest but her father never noticed. What Basil really wanted was to attend Dalton Black's culinary school and become a chef but Lloyd wouldn't know that because he never asked.

"You'll have to ask him." She looked down at her dad and shook her head. "Oh, about those sons... You've got five daughters who will one day bring men home. Be the man they look up to and respect." She leaned over and kissed his head. "Be the man I can respect. Somewhere along the way, you lost him, and I hope you find him soon. Time waits for no one."

She entered the house and bad went to worse. Her mom had rolled out of her chair and lay on the floor.

She rushed over to her. "Mom, are you okay?" She rolled her to her back and saw the blood crusted on her nose.

In a whisper, her mom said, "I'm glad you're home. I've never liked sleeping on the floor."

Awash with guilt for being late and spending needless minutes arguing with her father, Poppy attempted to lift her mother to her chair, but the task was impossible.

"Dad," she yelled. "Dad, help me."

Lloyd rushed into the house and saw his wife on the floor, the remnants of a bloody nose smeared across her upper lip.

He gave Poppy a look that said, "You should have been here."

They picked her up and put her back into her chair.

Poppy hated strapping her in but this was what happened when they didn't. She buckled her mom to the chair and went to the kitchen for a wet towel to clean her up.

Her father followed. Worry etched his eyes. "Poppy, if you had been—"

"No, don't say it. I already feel guilty." She wet a kitchen towel with warm water. "Where were you? Why was she alone? Oh, that's right, you were with your cows. Correction, you were waiting outside for me so you could tell me how being late was irresponsible. Where in the hell is Violet?" She wanted to yell every word at him but didn't. What was the point?

"Helping your brother move the herd. I'd only stepped out for ten minutes. I needed a break."

She knew the truth. He'd left her alone because most days she was okay, but not today.

"You're so damn selfish." She brushed past him to clean up her mom.

He leaned on the counter and watched from afar.

When Poppy returned to rinse the towel she said, "I'm calling in a nurse. She needs full-time care. None of us are qualified." She looked over her shoulder to where her mother sat. "She lost control of her bladder. Go take care of your wife. She needs you."

He swallowed like he was choking on her words. "I can't remember her like this. It breaks my heart."

"Then you don't deserve to remember her at all." Poppy pulled out her phone and dialed. "Sage, I need your help."

CHAPTER EIGHT

Mark entered the office dragging. Yesterday, he'd experienced the highest of highs with the kiss and the lowest of lows waiting for Poppy's call.

Aiden walked in minutes later. "You okay?"

Obviously, his disappointment was hard to hide. "I was thinking about Poppy."

Aiden walked to his desk and took a seat. "Terrible thing."

Mark was confused. How did he know Poppy hadn't called him? "I agree."

"What a shock it had to be to find her mom on the floor bleeding."

Mark lost his balance and gripped the edge of Aiden's desk. "Wait. What?"

"I'm talking about Carol falling out of her wheelchair and busting her nose on the floor. Carpet isn't much of a cushion when you take a header."

"When did that happen?"

"Yesterday afternoon." Aiden leaned back and kicked his feet up on his desk. "Poppy told Sage she was late getting home. The poor girl feels so bad, but hell, Lloyd was on the porch and didn't hear a thing."

Relief. Anger. Sadness. All three emotions hit him at once. "Is Carol all right?" It was a silly question. No one with ALS was all right.

Guilt seeped deep into his being. All night long he'd had a pity party for himself because Poppy hadn't called. All along it was because she was overwhelmed. He should have been there. He should be there for her now.

"What are they going to do? The family needs help but that stubborn ass won't allow anyone in since my dad screwed him over."

Aiden kicked off the desk and stood. "It's a damn shame. So many years wasted. What was that, twenty years ago?"

"Twenty-two. I was eight when my father left." Mark pulled out his phone, considering whether he should call Poppy or not.

"That was not your fault. You know that, right?"

"Yep, but I'll never convince Lloyd of that."

"Have you ever tried? I'm not talking about making up for what your father lacked but showing the man what you're made of."

Mark looked at Poppy's empty desk. She wasn't scheduled to come in for two days, but she was missed every day.

Aiden approached Mark and patted him on the back. "Doc and Sage are taking some supplies to the Dawsons' Ranch. They might need some help. Can you take over what they need? Since the stubborn ass, as you called him, is too proud to ask for help and too broke to afford home health care, the town is circling their wagons. Should have happened long ago if you ask me."

"You want me to drive supplies to the Dawsons?"

"Do you remember when Marina was struggling with everything and I had to take all that time off and you covered for me?"

He remembered it well. There were days when he'd worked around the clock, but he'd do it again because Aiden was like family. "I'd do it again, boss."

"It's my time to return the favor. Go and make sure your girl is okay. See what they need beyond medical help. I'm not great in the saddle, but I can clean out stalls and bale hay or whatever else those damn cowboys do. Part of your job is watching after the community. I'll expect a list tomorrow of things we can do to help the Dawsons get through this rough patch."

"A list? You know Lloyd isn't going to take charity."

Aiden laughed. "We're not offering charity. We're offering friendship. You make sure he knows the difference." Aiden patted him on the back the way a father would. "Give your girl a hug from all of us and tell her we'll miss her but not to hurry back to work."

Mark smiled. "She is my girl."

Aiden chuckled. "After that kiss on the street yesterday, no one would argue with you." He about pushed Mark from the door. "I'll see you tomorrow. Call me if you need anything." A hint of mischief danced in his eyes. "Wait a sec." Aiden went to the supply cabinet and pulled out a bulletproof vest. He pushed it into Marks hands. "Just in case."

Mark tossed the heavy thing back at him. "I've got my own in the cruiser. Besides, I'm going to kill him with kindness."

"Hope that works before he kills you with buckshot."

Mark walked away not sure if he should laugh or worry. He went straight to Doc's office and loaded up the supplies

Doc Parker, Dr. Covington and Sage would need to properly care for Carol. Sage went through her supply list twice before she said he could leave.

Instead of heading straight out, Mark stopped at Maisey's Diner to pick up several orders of fried chicken with all the fixings and made an additional stop at the corner store for flowers. No doubt Poppy could use a little pick-me-up.

THE DAWSONS' ranch was located south of town. He had to wind through a narrow country road to get to the turnoff to the Big D ranch. As kids, they'd laughed at the name. Neither Basil nor his sisters had escaped high school unscathed. Not a day had gone by when someone didn't ask one of them if they liked the big D.

Mark had thrown a lot of punches back then when the guys dared to talk to Poppy about their big Ds. The only big D he wanted Poppy to think about was his. That started him on thoughts about her dating life. At twenty-eight, she'd surely had a D or two. The thought soured his stomach but then again, it wasn't like he was virgin material. He'd had a grand old time when he attended training in Denver.

It had been apparent by then that Poppy would never cross her father, and a future together was impossible. Since he'd become a deputy, he'd had a few dates. A few hookups out of Copper Creek and a one night stand he regretted from Cross Creek.

He drove over the metal grates and approached the house with care. Lloyd was on the porch. The man grew before his eyes when he realized it was Mark in the cruiser and not Aiden. No one messed with Aiden.

No guns were present, so he opened the door and stepped onto the gravel.

"You don't belong here, son." The words were there but there didn't seem to be much conviction behind them. Exhaustion must have tempered Lloyd's disposition.

"I didn't come to see you. I'm dropping off supplies for Doc, Lydia, and Sage."

Lloyd's huff was drawn out and loud. He nodded with resignation. "I appreciate their help."

How hard could it be for the damn man to say thanks to Mark for making the run? Mark had to remind himself this wasn't for Lloyd. It was for Carol. It was also for Poppy because she needed support. No doubt she didn't get much from anyone at home.

"You want to help me carry it all in?" He knew his lips were stretched into a thin line. It was the only way he wouldn't frown.

"Yep, I'll give you a hand so you can leave. Poppy might have a soft spot in her heart for you, but I never will."

"I can live with that. What I can't live without is your daughter. I'm making my intentions known. I plan to court Poppy, and when the time is right, I'll make her mine for good." Mark's heart thumped so hard he was certain his ribs would crack. He'd never stood up to Lloyd but that was probably the problem, while he thought he was being respectful, all he was being, was stupid.

He opened the tail of the cruiser and they unloaded the boxes. Mark brought them to the steps and Lloyd took them inside. He craned his neck to get a glimpse of Poppy, but she wasn't anywhere in sight.

"She's bathing her mom," Lloyd said.

"Carol okay?" They went back to the cruiser. The only

thing left was the meal he'd picked up from Maisey's and the flowers.

"As good as can be expected." He looked past Mark's shoulders to the colorful buds. It was a mixed bouquet that had a little of everything from roses to gerbera daisies. "Waste of money," he grumbled.

Mark looked inside. "You talking about the flowers or the food?"

"Food is fine." He nodded toward the flowers.

Leave it to Lloyd to think a gift was a waste of money. "When was the last time you gave Carol flowers?"

Lloyd frowned. "Never. Why spend ten bucks on flowers when I could buy feed?"

Mark shook his head. "I'm not trying to be disrespectful. When I was a boy, I used to look up to you. I remember thinking you had it all. A big house. A lot of land. A nice wife. A beautiful daughter. I wanted to be you when I grew up, but I'm so glad I'm not." He grabbed the flowers. "These will bring a smile to her face. What value do you put on that? Joy and happiness are priceless."

Lloyd stared at him for a long minute. His shoulders wilted forward. "I never considered that type of return on my investment."

Though Mark had bought the flowers for Poppy, in that moment he knew Carol needed them more. No woman should die without ever receiving a proper bouquet. He pulled a single red rose from the center and pressed the rest into Lloyds hands. "Give it a try. It's never too late to get that smile."

He looked down at the flowers. "This time it is. She can't smile. Hell, she barely talks anymore." He tried to hand them back, but Mark shook his head.

"Her eyes will smile. Watch them and you'll know."

Mark picked up the food and followed Lloyd into the house. It had been a long time since he'd spent any time there. Not much had changed. The plaid couch still sat centered against the wall flanked by brown recliners that had seen better days. The place was spotless, but the outdated furnishings made it look dingy.

The box in his hand grew heavy. "Can I put this in the kitchen?"

Lloyd nodded. "Who do I owe?"

"No one. It's a gift."

"From who?"

Mark knew if he claimed responsibility, the damn man would toss the food away. "The food came from Maisey's."

How hard was it for him to accept a helping hand? "Tell her thanks."

Before he could say anything else, Poppy wheeled her mom down the hallway. Poor Carol had two black eyes, which meant she'd broken her nose.

When Poppy saw Mark, she stopped. Her eyes flashed from her father to him.

"I brought the supplies Doc thought you'd need. He said he'll stop by after clinic hours."

She let out a held breath. "That's great." She moved her hands to her hair, trying to brush it back from her face. She was a mess, but she was beautiful. "Thank you for bringing the supplies."

She stared at the flowers in her father's hands. "Are those for Mom?" She looked at Mark, a tear slipping from her eye.

"Yes, your father asked me to pick them up." Mark stepped behind Lloyd and gave him a little shove forward.

Lloyd walked to his wife and kneeled in front of her chair. "They're not as beautiful as you are, sweetheart, and they're about thirty years too late but I love you. I always have and I always will."

Happiness flickered in Carol's eyes. She whispered, "I love you too," then sat back and said the word "water" to Poppy.

"You're thirsty?"

In the slightest motion, Carol's head moved back and forth. It would have been almost imperceptible if they hadn't all been watching her so closely.

"The flowers," Mark said. "She wants water for the flowers."

A single nod was all Poppy needed to race into the kitchen, pulling Mark with her.

Once they were out of sight, she leaned her head against his chest. "I'm so sorry I didn't call. It's been..."

"It's been a helluva two days," he said.

She pulled a green vase out from under the sink. "Who would have thought you'd be standing in my kitchen."

"I'm not giving up, Poppy. I told your father the same thing."

Her eyes widened and her brows lifted. "What did he say?"

Mark chuckled. "Nothing, but he didn't shoot me."

"I'd say it's been a banner day." She gave him a quick peck on the lips before she returned to her mother. Poppy arranged the flowers and put them on the table. "You brought food too?"

"Can't have you getting sick before our first date on Friday." They both looked at Lloyd, who now sat beside Carol. The furrow between his brows was as deep as a canyon.

Carol whispered something. Lloyd leaned in to hear her better.

"What did she say?" Poppy asked.

Lloyd's features pruned up. "She said it was about time." While Poppy's father wasn't pleased about their date, the light in Carol's eyes said she was.

Poppy asked him to stay for dinner, much to Lloyd's distress.

Mark asked her to take a walk with him first.

She looked at her parents. "Is that okay with you?"

Her father rolled his eyes. "You're a grown woman. You don't need my permission."

"You're right." She threaded her fingers through Mark's and walked him out the front door. There was a story there. A story he wanted to hear after he got a kiss or ten.

CHAPTER NINE

Hand in hand, Mark led her to the back of his cruiser. The tailgate still hung open with a single red rose lying on the plastic liner.

He picked it up and gave it to her.

"Thank you." She brought it to her nose and breathed in the sweet scent. "And thanks for the flowers for my mom."

He smiled. "I didn't give them to her."

She laughed. "We both know my father well enough to know he didn't buy them. He'd never spring for flowers when he could buy chicken feed."

She watched Mark shake with laughter. "While I don't want to take credit for the flowers in any way, that was exactly what he said when he saw them. Told me they were a waste."

It broke her heart that her mother got so little in the way of romance. Poppy wanted more. With the reality of her mother's imminent death came the reality of Poppy's life. She was tired of living by someone else's standards. Reaching for someone else's dreams.

"Did you really want a tour of the ranch or was that your way of getting me alone to steal kisses."

He peeked around the cruiser to see if her father was on the porch or looking out the window. Without letting her go, he walked to the driver's side, opened the door, and reached in to get a pen and a notebook.

He turned around and pulled her in for a hug. "Kisses sound amazing, but I don't want to have to steal them. I hope you'll give them to me freely."

She stepped back and glanced at the paper and pen. "Are you taking notes on our kisses?"

She loved the dimples that appeared on his cheeks when he smiled. The way his eyes lit up when he was happy. Usually a rich dark brown like high-end chocolate, they took on amber highlights that danced with mischief.

"No notes on kisses. Those I'm storing in my memory." He tapped his head. "I'm cataloging each one as the best kiss ever." He placed his hand on her lower back and started to walk toward the barn. He raised the pen and paper. "This is official business."

She tilted her head. There was nothing going on at the ranch that required the law. "I don't understand."

"Your father is stubborn."

"You think?"

"I know, and so does the rest of the town, that he needs help but won't ask for it. He's full of pride."

"He's full of something," she jested.

"Aiden asked me to take some notes on stuff that needs to be done around the ranch and so that's what I'm going to do. I would have asked your father but we're barely on speaking terms and he would have told me he didn't need anything."

"You're right." They reached the barn and walked

inside. It smelled like wet hay, dust, and chicken shit. "I learned something yesterday."

"That I'm an excellent kisser and a better catch?" he teased.

"There was that, but I learned that my dad will back down if challenged. I never considered fighting him on anything until I got home yesterday and he was sitting on the porch pissed that I was late."

Mark turned to her and cupped her cheek with his free hand. "I'm so sorry I made you late and got you in trouble."

"You didn't." She lifted her shoulders. "You actually did but, honestly, why at twenty-eight should I be getting in trouble. I live at my parents' house because they need me to not because I want to." She walked to a bale of hay and took a seat. Mark followed. "I pushed back on my father yesterday. I told him you were the man for me."

His eyes grew wide. "What did he say?"

"He said you weren't good for me and would never be his choice."

Mark's shoulders drooped. "He may not ever like me, but I'm going to earn his respect."

She leaned sideways and touched her head to his shoulder. Mark wasn't a lumberjack of a man, but he wasn't of slight build either. His shoulders were wide enough to carry the burdens of his life. His chest was big enough to hold a large and compassionate heart.

"You don't have to impress him. You have to impress me."

She lifted the rose she'd carried all the way here. The head of the flower had begun to droop, but she didn't care. It was the prettiest flower in the world. "This is the first flower I've ever received from a man."

He pressed his lips to hers. "It won't be your last."

"I'm glad. Isn't it silly how long we've waited to act on our attraction to one another?"

"You think I'm attracted to you?"

His lips twitched, which meant he was messing with her. It was as if his lips laughed before his brain gave the signal.

She could give as good as she got. "Not really. I imagine you're feeling the same as me." She lifted herself from the hay bale and walked away. "Taking one for the team so to speak. I mean...someone has to love you. You know the town motto, 'we take care of our own.'"

His mouth dropped open. "Oh, so yesterday was a mercy kissing. A single kiss to put me out of my lonely man's misery?"

She couldn't help the eye roll. "Of course, what else would it be?"

He lifted and stalked toward her. "What else indeed." With his body pushed against hers, he walked her backward until she hit the old worn wood of the barn. The rough weathered texture pressed into her skin. "So sorry you had to suffer through that kiss." He looked deep into her eyes.

She raised her arms and wrapped them around his neck. "It was a terrible hardship to have your perfect lips touch mine. To taste you and have you moan into my mouth. Such a personal sacrifice, Mark." She leaned forward and brushed her lips across his. It was a good thing he had her pinned against the wall because his kisses weakened her knees. "I'll happily be the town martyr when it comes to you."

"Is that right?"

"Yes, I've been waiting for you all my life."

"Wait no more, sweetheart." He covered her mouth with his. Soft licks of their tongues. Little nips of their teeth.

Their bodies pressed closely together, it was hard to tell where he stopped and she began.

It was at least five minutes before they broke apart. Her lips were swollen. Her breath ragged. Her core clenched from desire. Her panties no doubt wet.

Mark was no better off than her. His chest heaved. His lips were deliciously red. His hair was mussed where she'd run her fingers through it.

"You have no idea what you do to me," he said in a gravelly voice that rippled down her spine and settled between her shaking legs.

She eyed the noticeable bulge in his trousers. "I've got some idea."

He adjusted himself and stepped back. "While I'd love to stay here and kiss you all day, I've got a list to make."

She nodded, knowing he was right. Getting naked and rolling in the hayloft sounded infinitely better than list making, but he had work to do and she needed to get back to the house and care for her mother.

"We should hurry and get your list finished. You brought a meal and it's getting cold."

He flipped the notebook open to a blank page. "What needs to be done?"

She rushed him around the main area of the ranch and pointed out items that needed attention from the chicken coop to the leak on the roof. She talked about how the lower pasture fence was falling apart and each week her father would repair a section only to have another go down.

"Sounds like your brother is spending more time chasing down runaway cattle than anything else."

"It's true. We're on a Ferris wheel we can't stop. Poor Violet spends more time in the saddle these days than anywhere else. She walks in each night so spent, she barely has the energy to eat."

He threaded his fingers through her hand and walked her back to the house. When they got there, her father was sitting on the porch.

"Is Mom secured?"

He spit his chew into the nearby bush. "Yep, she told me to wait outside for you two to return."

"Why?" Poppy asked.

Her father looked like he might choke on his chew. He stood and kicked the gravel around with his boots.

"*She'd* like you to stay for dinner, deputy." His nose scrunched as if he was breathing in something foul like days-old roadkill. He leaned over the tobacco-stained bush and unloaded his lip.

Poppy was so happy Mark didn't have that nasty habit. She realized everyone had their vices and chewing tobacco was preferable to alcohol abuse, but she'd never be able to smell wintergreen and not think about the amount of spit that poor bush took in.

"Thank you for the invite, but I need to get back."

"I didn't invite you. Carol did."

Poppy squeezed Mark's hand. "You should stay. I mean you did bring the meal, you should enjoy it."

Her father grumbled. "He brought it, not bought it." He headed up the steps. "Stop kissing my daughter on company time. That's not what my tax dollars pay for."

She felt Mark stiffen behind her. She leaned in and whispered, "Remember, he's more bark than bite."

"I'm on call all the time, Mr. Dawson. I'd have to wait until I retired to kiss Poppy by your standards."

At the door, Lloyd turned and said, "That suits me fine."

"It doesn't suit me."

Poppy walked him to the cruiser. "He'll come around."

Mark shook his head. "No, he won't, but hey, I don't need to impress him. I only need to impress you."

She wrapped her arms around him. "That's right. And I am impressed." She lifted on tiptoes and brushed his lips with hers. "What's been your favorite kiss so far?"

He pulled her closer. Tucked out of sight by the driver's door, he gave her a quick peck that wasn't enough. "This one," he said as he gave her a kiss she'd remember forever.

"I'm still counting on lunch for Wednesday if you can get away," he told her as he opened the door and climbed inside.

"I'll get away if you're buying lunch and giving kisses."

He smiled that glittering, mischievous smile. "I'm willing to take one for the team."

CHAPTER TEN

When Mark got back to town, Aiden was gone and everything but Bishop's Brewhouse was locked up tight for the day.

When he entered the Brewhouse, Cannon was pulling a beer for Luke Mosier, who sat by himself at the bar.

Mark took a seat several down from the fireman.

Cannon slid Luke's across the bar and grabbed Mark a cup of coffee. He never drank in uniform. It wasn't professional and while Aiden would have allowed it, Mark would never do it. He had a lot to make up for in this town and most of it had nothing to do with him.

"Thanks," he said as Cannon set the steaming mug in front of him.

"You look good for a dead man."

It didn't take a genius to figure out what he meant. "Lloyd wasn't armed when I showed up. Besides, I brought dinner and supplies. It would have been unwise to kill me before the cruiser was unloaded."

"Always knew Lloyd was a thinker."

Mark shook his head. "Doesn't think much of me."

Luke picked up his beer and moved two stools down so he sat next to Mark. "I hear you've been kissing my girl."

Mark's frown tightened every muscle in his face. He wasn't one to fight, but he wasn't going to give Poppy up easily now that he knew her intentions.

"Your affection is misguided. Poppy is mine. Always has been, and always will be." His commanding tone surprised everyone, himself included. Something powerful and possessive came over him. He felt like a hungry dog and Poppy was the bone. Except she was far prettier.

"Glad you figured it out. Everyone around town is tired of you two orbiting each other and not acting on the attraction pulling you together." Luke took a long draw of his beer. "I haven't been here for long and I'm already tired of it myself."

"So, you're not interested in Poppy?" Mark needed to know who his competition was.

"I don't fish in another man's pond or poach on his land. It's common knowledge in town that Poppy has a thing for you."

Mark wished his coffee was a beer or a whiskey or both but it was coffee so he took a sip and studied the man in front of him. "At the wedding, you said you were spending the afternoon with the prettiest girl in town."

Luke chuckled. "I was. Poppy is the prettiest single girl in town."

"She's not single," grumbled Mark.

"That's apparent. It was obvious that day when all she could talk about was you." Luke moved the bowl of bar snacks in front of him and picked out the peanuts, eating them one by one.

"She talked about me?"

Luke shook his head. "All damn night. Did you know

70

half the photos on her camera are of you? The damn woman is worse than the paparazzi with a long lens."

Poppy loved taking pictures. It was her passion. She had been taking them for years. At first, it was with those disposable cameras, and then one year her mother got her a used Nikon. Going digital allowed her to take hundreds of pictures without the added expense of developing and printing.

Mark's chest puffed with pride. "Only half?" he teased.

"Well, you did leave the wedding early."

"Yeah, man, you left my reception."

Mark felt guilty because he had bailed on his friend's celebration. "I'm sorry about that. It was so hard to watch all my married friends and look at Poppy so happy sitting next to Luke." He turned to Luke. "You're her father's wet dream."

"Dude, that's disgusting."

Mark grabbed the bowl of bar snacks and dumped a pile of the nuts and cracker mix in front of him before Luke could eat all the peanuts.

"It's true. You're the fire chief. You have a house. You grew up on a ranch. You're a dad's billion-dollar lottery win."

"Hmm," Luke said, as he pushed the bar mix away. "Let's get this straight. I'm the fire chief, you're a police deputy. I'd say that's even. Both public servants. Both in respectable professions. I've got a house, but so do you. Mine is old and in need of repairs. Yours looks in better shape."

"You've seen my house?"

Luke laughed. "I need to know everyone's house by name here. My first week I got a call that said there was a fire at old man Tucker's house. I didn't know who the hell

71

he was. Had to ask Doc where to go. No one had a clue what the address was, so I've been memorizing who lives where."

"I didn't hear about Zachariah's house being on fire," Cannon took Luke's mug and topped it off before he did the same for Mark's coffee.

"Me either," Mark said.

"Turns out it wasn't his house, but one of his stills. The damn man is going to burn down the whole mountainside with his bootlegging. Can't you do something about that? Isn't it illegal to make your own mash?"

"Not really. It's not illegal to make alcohol. What is illegal is to sell it without a license, but Tucker doesn't sell anything, he barters and bartering isn't illegal either. It's very much like the new marijuana laws. It's not illegal to grow your own as long as you don't exceed your plant limit. It is illegal to sell it, but you can give it away. I can't arrest Tucker for bringing a case of moonshine to Doc. I can't arrest Doc for seeing to Tucker's health for free."

Luke shook his head. "The stuff will burn a hole right through your gut."

Cannon pulled up a stool behind the bar and took a seat. "So, you've been the recipient of Tucker's kindness too?" He reached below the counter and brought up a mason jar filled with crystal clear liquid.

"Yep, it was his gift to the station for putting out what he called a kitchen fire. That would be true if his kitchen was outside in the middle of the woods."

"Small towns. They have their own rules." Mark always thought it funny that a bootlegger who lived in a shack in the hills got more respect from Lloyd Dawson than he did.

"How are things at the Dawsons'?" Cannon asked.

"Sage and Doc drove out there a bit ago to see to Carol. I hear she's taken a turn for the worse."

"She looks rough, but she did take a significant fall yesterday. I made a list of things the Dawsons needed." He pulled his small notebook from his shirt pocket and flipped it open. "The ranch needs some work."

On some level, Mark felt responsible for getting the ranch in shape. It was his father's actions that made Lloyd close himself off to the idea of help. He'd replaced the ranch hands with his kids. They had effectively become slave labor because of one man's actions.

"Let me see that list." Luke slid the notebook toward himself. He thumbed down line by line. "Fences and chicken coops are right up my alley. I can definitely help with those."

This was a moment when Mark would have to decide if he'd let jealousy or compassion rule his world. Luke's presence on the ranch would put him in a place of notice. Even though Poppy made it clear she was actively pursuing Mark, he didn't much want Luke around to change her mind. But facts were facts, the Dawsons needed help desperately, and his insecurities had to be set aside.

"That would be great. The place is falling down around them. Anything you can do will be appreciated."

"Why did they let it get this bad before they asked for help?"

Mark wasn't sure if he should tell the truth. Lloyd's disdain for him wasn't a secret around town, but how was he supposed to get past it if he had to relive it. Then again, how could he get past it if he couldn't explain it and put it to rest? For the next fifteen minutes, he told Luke the story of how his father had driven the Dawsons' thriving cattle ranch into the ground overnight.

"Oh wow, you've got an uphill battle to fight."

"Don't I know it." He reached into his pocket for a five and laid it on the table.

Cannon shoved it back to him. "You know coffee is on the house. How can I sell something that looks like grease and tastes worse?"

Mark shook his head. "If you don't want my money, then put it in a jar and start a fund for the Dawsons. One day not too far in the future, they're going to have to bury Carol and I don't think they're prepared for that."

All three men lowered their heads as if in prayer.

Cannon pulled an empty mason jar from under the counter. Apparently, he'd had a few gifts from old man Tucker himself if the moonshine jar was any indicator. He shoved the five inside and set it by the register. "I'll put a label on it later."

"When will Lloyd be expecting help?" Luke asked.

That was another battle to fight. Another hill to climb.

"He won't be expecting it. In fact, I'm certain he'll fight it every second of the way, but he's getting help regardless." Mark picked up his notepad and tucked it into his pocket. "This is Aspen Cove, and we take care of our own no matter how stubborn and asinine they are."

"If fences need fixing, we're going to need supplies. Is there anyone who can donate wood, nails, and wire?"

Mark hadn't thought much about supplies. Volunteers were fine, but they wouldn't be effective if they didn't have the things they required to do the job. In his desire to help, he'd put the cart in front of the horse.

On his way home, he stopped at Aiden's to show him the list and tell him he was going to round up supplies. Aiden patted him on the back and told him he was proud of the work he'd done.

How long had it been since anyone had told him they were proud? Why did it matter so much for him to have the approval of others? He knew it all came down to the fateful day more than two decades ago. The day his father changed lives. How could a man abandon his wife and son?

An ache, as painful as what he imagined a heart attack would feel like, gripped his chest. He'd never considered the effect of abandonment on him. He'd simply tried to ease his mom's pain and taken Lloyd Dawson's dirty looks and comments and swallowed them down. The problem was at the age of eight he'd been a sponge and soaked in all those negative thoughts, and somewhere inside himself, he believed them. That would have to stop.

"I am not my father," he said as he marched up the walkway of the big Victorian where Wes Covington and his wife Lydia lived. Mark was a man of integrity and a man of action unless you counted his attraction to Poppy. He'd let her slip between his fingers because he'd been fed the message that he wasn't worthy. "Screw that," he mumbled as he knocked on the door.

If anyone could procure building materials, it would be the town's resident builder. Surely, he'd have connections.

An hour later he left the Covington house with a sense of accomplishment and pride. All it took was a phone call from Wes to Noah Lockhart, the oldest of the Lockhart brothers who'd built the Guild Creative Center, to get what he'd need. Turned out he had a connection to the Stevenson Lumber Mill in Cross Creek and after a few more calls, Mark had everything he'd need to get the projects started. All that was left was to convince Lloyd that he could be trusted around the ranch to do the right thing and not steal what was left.

CHAPTER ELEVEN

It was Wednesday, and Poppy was meeting Mark for lunch.

Violet was riding in from the range to relieve her soon. After Mom's fall, no one left her unattended. It was too risky. Even her father was spending more time with her. Each time he left Poppy watched his shoulders curl forward. His height seemed to diminish. While she knew watching his wife die had to be hard, she also knew he'd regret the time he spent running from the truth. Carol Dawson was going to die.

Each time she thought about it, her throat tightened, and her stomach turned, but she couldn't focus on her mom's death when she still had some life to live. Her mother's minutes were precious and should be spent with those who loved her, including her stubborn husband.

Mark's visit seemed like a lifetime ago and yet it took him no time to organize the help he promised. This morning, a truck from the Stevenson Mill showed up and delivered materials that Lockhart construction donated.

It took all Poppy had in her to not rope and tie her father to a beam in the barn. He stood outside, shaking his head and telling the delivery driver to take his charity somewhere else. If it weren't for her brother Basil telling them where to stack the wood, she was certain her dad would have succeeded in running them off. He was minutes away from grabbing his shotgun when Violet rode over and told him a section of the south fence had collapsed overnight. At that point, he couldn't turn down the wood he needed to repair it.

"Go get your man," her mother whispered. Her voice had grown so wispy and weak that it was really her yell. Each word took so much out of her. It was heartbreaking to watch this powerful woman who had given birth to and raised six children wither in front of her. One thing that boosted her mom's spirits was the possibility that love could be blooming between Poppy and Mark.

A goofy grin took over Poppy's face. "He is kind of my man, huh?"

"Always has been," her mother said before she closed her eyes. That was the way of it these days. Everything from speaking to breathing was like moving mountains.

Poppy brushed the hair from her mom's face and raised the hospital bed frame so her mother wouldn't accidentally fall out.

She brought the cup of broth she'd been feeding her mom into the kitchen. Since Monday, their living room had been transformed into a nursing home. A hospital bed had been delivered and set up where the sofa used to be. Someone, whether it be Doc, Lydia, or Sage, came to check on her mother daily.

The best thing about small towns was everyone was family regardless of actual genetics. It was never more evident than the outpouring of love that came in the form of casseroles, savory broth for her mother, haircuts for the family from Sheriff Cooper's wife, Marina, wood from a local lumber mill, and free labor.

Poppy dried her hands on a kitchen towel and walked to the hallway mirror to make sure she was ready for her date. While it wasn't the kind of first date she'd dreamed of having with Mark, it was the first time they would meet up as an actual couple.

Her sister came running into the back door as a light knock sounded at the front door. "That's Luke," Violet said as she shed her boots by the back door and disappeared down the hallway to the bathroom.

Poppy shook her head at her sister. She was only eighteen and seemed to run around like her hair was on fire. Then again at eighteen, even Poppy remembered feeling like everything in her life was happening so fast. It didn't help when both of her parents' favorite saying was something about daylight burning, or time's a wasting, or time waiting for no man.

"Hey Luke," Poppy said as she opened the door.

The tall and handsome firefighter stood in front of her dressed in worn jeans, work boots, and a tattered T-shirt. If she hadn't been so focused on Mark, she would have been attracted to Luke. He didn't make her heart ache or her lips tingle for kisses but that was probably because she hadn't pined after him since she was a child.

"Poppy, you're looking nice." He smiled as his eyes moved over her. There wasn't any hint in his expression that he found her intriguing or attractive. He simply looked at her like her brother did when they used to dress up for special occasions. "You got a date?" He lifted a brow.

She looked over her shoulder to see her sister take the recliner that sat next to their mom. Stepping outside, she moved across the porch and leaned on the rail.

"As a matter of fact, I do. I'm having lunch with Mark."

His broad smile made her feel all warm inside. "I think that's great. I'm glad, he seems like a good man."

Poppy nodded. "He is a good man." She'd known him her whole life. Everything he did was good from the way he shoveled snow from his neighbor's driveway in the winter to the way he doted on Aiden's daughter Kellyn when she made him sit for long bouts of time so she could perfect her stick figure drawings of him. "Thanks for sitting next to me at the wedding."

He made a silly face, one where his eyeballs moved in two different directions. "It was a real sacrifice to sit next to a beautiful woman and try to make a knucklehead get jealous."

They both chuckled. "Speaking of knuckleheads, here comes my father. He's going to try to make you leave, but I'm going to ask you to stay. Just in case you've heard about his sharpshooter skills, you should know that I've unloaded his shotgun and hid his ammo."

"Good to know. Thanks for looking out after me."

It was her turn to make a face. She rolled her eyes and pursed her lips. "It was more about me than you—actually more about Mark in case he set foot on our land again."

Her father stomped his boots on the first step to loosen the mud and muck from the bottoms.

"Luke, good to see you." He offered his hand for a shake.

"I've got the day off and heard you might need some help with the fences."

Poppy held her breath, waiting for her father's displeasure. She wondered if it would come out in a rash of unpleasant words aimed at offending Luke, or if it would be dealt in a single sentence that ended with "get off my land."

"I'm grateful for the help."

Poppy shook her head. "Wait. What?" She couldn't believe her ears. "Did you say *grateful?*"

Her father frowned. "How's your mother?"

"Asleep," she said. "Violet's with her."

"Good." Lloyd pointed to the south pasture. "I've got a fence down, and I could really use a hand."

"I've got two." Luke skipped down the steps in front of Lloyd.

"Now that's a good man, Poppy."

A thread of frustration worked its way through her. "Yes, Dad, he is. A good man who's here to help because another good man asked him to. Stop being as bullheaded as one of your steers."

"You're not too old for me to ground."

"Yes, I am." She opened the door and reached in for her purse and keys. "I'll be back."

"Where are you off to now?"

She wanted to growl or hit him upside the head with her purse. "I'm having lunch with Mark. You knew that. I told you already."

"Your mom says I have a selective memory."

"She's got you pegged."

Poppy hopped into the cab of the old truck. She pumped the gas five times and turned the key. It coughed and sputtered and then roared to life. She put it in gear and drove forward only to have the beast backfire. In her rearview mirror, she watched both her father and Luke nearly hit the ground like she'd shot them.

She laughed for the whole twenty minutes it took her to get to Maisey's Diner. Her father wasn't so bad after all. Like Mark, he'd been labeled as stubborn and mean, when in fact he was vulnerable. Everyone had a shell they showed the world.

She walked into the diner and found Mark sitting at the corner booth. He was quickly shedding his protective shield. He wasn't a man who wouldn't fight for what he wanted. He was simply a man who needed to be reminded of what that something was.

When he looked up from his phone and smiled at her she was reminded of why she'd fallen for him all those years ago. There was strength in his eyes and a tenderness to his smile.

He stood and walked to her like she was a light and he was a bug.

"Gorgeous." He leaned in and kissed her cheek.

"Handsome," she said and turned to kiss him. It was a sweet, innocent kiss that she let linger for the longest time, until Maisey walked over.

"You want something to drink for when you're done sucking that boy's face off?" Maisey asked.

She moved away and saw how handsome Mark looked in a blush. "I'll take a lemonade."

He placed his hand on the small of her back and led the way to the corner booth, where a bouquet of flowers sat in her seat.

"For me?" She picked them up and brought them to her nose. They were a mix of flowers but in the center was another single red rose.

"You don't see me kissing anyone else, do you?"

"I better not. I just got you. I'm not ready to give you up."

"You'll never have to give me up. I'm yours, Poppy, for as long as you'll have me."

She slid into the booth and set the flowers on the table.

"The question is...how long will you have me?" She was sadly inexperienced when it came to all things men. Her knowledge about relationships came from the Hallmark Channel or the books she managed to pick up on her occasional trips to Copper Creek.

While she did have a date or two in high school and a few during the time Mark had been away at training, she couldn't call herself worldly or wise. At twenty-eight she was still a virgin. That one time with Eddie Pierce at the Copper Creek 4H show a few years ago couldn't count. She'd been determined to lose her virginity before she turned twenty-five so when they shared a bottle of whiskey and she climbed into the horse trailer with him that was the only thing on her mind. Sadly, he'd finished before they'd really gotten started. All she got was a hangover and an embarrassed apology.

"What are you thinking about?"

She had a habit of speaking without thinking. "Sex." Earlier she'd thought Mark looked cute when his skin blushed pink. He looked even sexier in the sheer rush of red that bloomed on his cheeks.

CHAPTER TWELVE

"Holy hell, Poppy. You can't just blurt out *sex* in the middle of the restaurant." He moved farther into the booth to hide his growing arousal. It was bad enough that she arrived wearing tight jeans and a tank top that hid none of her ample assets, but when the word *sex* left her lips, he became as hard as concrete.

"I know I'm not supposed to blurt it out, but it's not against the law. If it is, I'd be interested in seeing how your cuffs felt on my wrists." She thrust her arms across the table as if she were surrendering. "Have you ever used them outside of work?" She lifted a brow and cracked a smile.

The woman was going to kill him. "No, but keep it up, and you'll be sorry you asked about my cuffs." He pulled them off his belt and set them on the table.

When she snapped her hands back to her lap, he wanted to laugh. One thing he knew about Poppy was she was more bark than bite. After his run-in with her father, he wondered if it was a family trait.

He changed the subject. "How's your mom today?"

"Tired, but she seems okay. She told me to come get my man."

He sat up and took pride in that statement. How long had he wanted to be her man? "I'm glad one of your parents likes me."

Poppy's eyes danced with mischief. The tiny specks of amber lit up like lanterns. "I'm pretty sure she was talking about Luke, who came by this morning to help my father."

When his jaw dropped, she reached across the table to lift his chin and close his mouth. "I'm teasing. She likes you. Always has. Don't forget, your mother and mine were close friends at one time. I'm pretty sure they'd planned our wedding and the dozen kids we'd have so the ranch would always be manned."

His head swam with thoughts. The first was how much he wanted to hate Luke but couldn't. The second was the word *wedding*. The most shocking was talk of a dozen kids. "You want a dozen?"

Before she could respond, Maisey brought Poppy's lemonade and topped off Mark's coffee. "What do you two want for lunch?" Maisey jotted down the burgers and fries they ordered and left.

Poppy sipped her lemonade and hummed.

Mark loved the sounds she made when she tasted something she liked. If she could get that happy over lemon juice, sugar, and water, he wondered how many sounds he could pull from her when they actually had sex. While he didn't have a belt notched with his conquests, he hadn't had any complaints to speak of.

When it looked like he and Poppy would never be able to act on their attraction, he'd left town to pursue a career in law enforcement. It was in Denver that he learned a lot of things like self-defense, close quarter combat, and how to drive a woman crazy with his tongue. He couldn't wait to put that education to work on Poppy.

"I was thinking at least three." She took her napkin and placed it on her lap.

"Three what?" he asked.

"Short attention span? You asked if I wanted a dozen kids."

"Oh, the kids. Thank God, I've only got a three-bedroom house. If you wanted a dozen, we'd have to bunk them six to a room or share ours which would make it hard to have a dozen."

He thought nothing of talking about their future together. It wasn't as if he hadn't closed his eyes and pictured it a thousand times.

"What if I'd said I wanted a dozen?"

He reached across the table and put his hands out for her to hold. When she laid her palms on top of his, he held them tight.

"While it's a little early to plan our family, considering we've only shared a few kisses, I would have been happy to entertain the idea of making twelve babies with you."

He watched her expression go from warm to wicked. That sly smile of hers giving it all away.

"Now *you're* talking about sex in public."

He tucked his chin and sat up straight. "I am not."

"Yes, you are," she said with false indignation. One of Poppy's favorite things was to get him riled. "You don't get twelve babies without a lot of sex. It's not like I can have a litter with one shot."

He let go of one of her hands and reached below the table to adjust his erection, now pressing hard into the zipper of his trousers.

They'd taken decades to get to this place in their relationship, the rest wouldn't be taking that long. He needed Poppy in his bed, naked with him pressed deeply inside her. If that started the first of their so-called litter, then so be it. He'd been in like, lust, and love with her since he could remember. Even when he'd been with others it was her smile he'd see, her green eyes that would look back at him.

"Poppy, if you don't stop talking about sex, I'm going to strip you naked and take you right here in this booth." It was his desire that spoke. The gentleman his mother raised would have never talked to her like that, but he loved the look of shock that covered her face. The way her mouth hung open and her tongue rimmed her lips. "Close your mouth, or I'll put it to good use as well."

She snapped her mouth closed, but he saw the heat and desire in her eyes. Her hips shifted on the seat, making him feel confident that she was experiencing the same type of discomfort he was moments ago.

"Here you two go." Maisey slid two plates filled with burgers and fries in front of them. If their appetite for each other couldn't be sated, they'd have to settle for junk food.

The rest of their date was toned down with talk moving from work that needed to be done at the ranch to the projects Mark was working on at his house.

"So, you refurbished the whole house yourself?" She pulled a fry through a lake of ketchup.

"It's a work in progress. You want to see it?" He was sure he could take a longer lunch since everything seemed to be quiet in town. Most days things were quiet now that the construction on the Guild Creative Center was complete. The extra workers the project brought in had moved on, which meant there were fewer bar fights, fewer fender benders, and fewer burglaries.

"Now?"

He pulled out his wallet and left thirty dollars on the table, which would cover the bill and a good tip.

"Yes, now would be fine. I've got time."

She picked up her flowers and her purse and slid out of the booth. "I haven't been in your house in twenty years at least."

"It's time for a tour then."

Rather than put her in the cruiser, he had her follow him to his house. He couldn't believe Poppy Dawson would be alone with him behind closed doors. He pulled onto Spruce Lane. It was one of a few streets not named after a flower in town. Funny for a town named after a tree.

He exited his SUV and rushed to her beat-up old truck to help her out. It was a wonder the thing started each time she turned the key. With the way it choked and coughed there was no doubt the timing was off.

"Don't look at the front. I'm repainting this year and then starting on the landscape as soon as the weather warms up."

She tucked her hands in the pockets of her jeans. Goosebumps rose on her arms. Were they from the slight chill in the air or from the prospect of walking inside his house?

"What color are you going to paint it?"

He took in the peeling olive drab color. Whoever had painted it last time hadn't put much thought into the color. If it had been his father, it was certainly chosen because it was on sale.

"Not sure. I was thinking of something brighter and happier."

"Oooh," she purred. "Like a butter yellow with white trim?"

He settled his hand at the small of her back and walked

her forward. His palm fell to the curve of her ass—an ass formed by hours in the saddle.

"Is that what you'd like to see?"

She leaned into him like it was the most natural thing to do, like walking into his house was something she'd done dozens of times.

"I think it would look great. That and flower boxes and flower beds. A picket fence out front to keep your litter of children under control," she teased.

He jingled the cuffs he'd placed back on his belt. "I've got cuffs. Or we could buy lots of duct tape and rope."

"I like how you think."

He unlocked the door and pushed it open. Outside of the construction mess, his place was tidy. He made his bed each morning. Washed and dried his dishes after each meal. He hung up his clothes, dusted his furniture, and took out his trash. He was a fully domesticated animal.

"Wow, I love the great room." She walked inside and stood in the center of his living room, which opened to the kitchen and dining space.

"You like it?" It was important to him that she did because deep down inside he knew that every nail he'd driven into the wood, every surface he'd sanded smooth, was for her.

"I love it." She twirled around in a circle. Her long hair chased her until she stopped and it fell in front of her face.

He pushed her hair back and cupped her cheek. "I've always wanted you here. Never thought it would happen."

She leaned into him, rubbing her cheek against his chest. "I never thought I'd be here either."

The truth sat heavy in the air.

"We were stupid."

She leaned back and laughed. "Speak for yourself. You were stupid. I've just been waiting for you to smarten up."

"I'm sorry I took so long." He bent down and covered her mouth with his. It started slow, sweet, and careful.

His chest ached, as if his heart was squeezed by a vise.

Her knees seemed wobbly as she sank into him like an ice cube melting into a puddle.

Rising on tiptoes to meet his kiss, she reciprocated with equal force and passion. This moment was long overdue. Something feral broke free and moved to the surface.

Before he knew it, his hands were cupping her breasts and hers were clawing at his back.

He moved her in reverse to the couch, where her knees buckled and she fell to the plush upholstery. His body followed and came to rest on top of hers.

It wasn't how he'd pictured their first real intimate encounter, but then again life was uncertain, and they had to take it as it came.

He whispered against her lips. "God, Poppy. I've waited for so damn long to have you."

She licked and nibbled at his lips. "Take me. I'm yours. I've always been yours."

The devil on his left shoulder cheered him on while the angel on his right shoulder told him he was on duty. It wasn't professional. She deserved more.

She shifted under him, her hand reaching between their bodies. "Billy club or you?" she asked out of breath.

"What?" He shook his head, trying to clear it and make sense of her words.

She unhooked his baton and tossed it to the floor. "You had me half-frightened to death."

He finally caught her meaning. "No need to be frightened. While I'm not bat big, I have enough to satisfy." At least he hoped that was true. He wasn't sure what Poppy was used to. He stood up and tabled his service weapon and his cuffs. The devil on his left was winning. One look at her lying on his couch with her lips kiss swollen, and nipples poking through the soft cotton of her shirt, he knew there was no going back.

"Have you had many?" Her words were a soft whisper that floated through the air. "I mean—"

"I won't kiss and tell, and I don't expect you to either. What's in the past is in the past. What's in the future is you."

She let out an exhale. "Sounds good."

"You want to continue where we left off or do you want to tour the rest of the house?"

She giggled. "I'm not finished exploring the couch."

He pressed a knee between her thighs and grabbed the hem of her T-shirt. "You're a girl after my own heart."

"I want more than your heart, Officer Bancroft."

He lifted the soft cotton over her head and took in the contrast of her pale skin against the black lace of her bra.

"So damn beautiful." He traced his lips over her soft skin, stopping to pluck at the hardened nubs poking against the lace. He'd been wrong about her sounds. Nothing would ever compare to the moan that slipped from her mouth the minute he rolled one tight bud between his lips.

"Ohhh," she exhaled. Her hands moved from his back to his butt and returned to his back. She pulled him down so he sat heavy and hard between her thighs.

"I want you, Poppy. So damn freaking bad." He reached behind her and unhooked her bra, letting her perfect breasts spill from their confinement. "Wow, as a teen I fantasized about these." He cupped them and ran his callused thumbs over skin that pebbled and puckered beneath his touch.

"Living up to the dream?"

He ran his tongue between the two. "Damn wet dream."

Her tiny fingers yanked his tie loose and worked at his buttons until his khaki shirt was loose and his T-shirt was bunched up to his armpits. She skated her fingertips against the hair on his chest.

"I always knew you'd be like this. Hard but soft."

He pressed his hips to hers. "When you're around I'm always hard."

"Is this really happening?"

He brushed his lips against hers. "Do you want this to happen?"

She nodded.

His hands took the long tour around her body, feeling the hardness of her thighs through denim and the softness of her breasts with nothing to hinder his progress.

"Feel good?"

She ran her hands through his hair. "I've never felt anything like it."

He chuckled. "I'm sure that's not true."

She lifted on her elbows and looked down at him. "No, you don't understand. You will be my first. I've read about —"

Mark bolted up like he'd been doused in ice water. "Your first?"

"Yep. Had I known, I would have asked for a tour sooner." She moved her hands to the button of his pants. "I want the extended tour." She giggled.

"No, we can't." He snapped his hand to his zipper. The devils on his shoulders argued over whether he should continue but there was no way he'd take Poppy's virginity on his couch. "I didn't know, Poppy, I'm sorry."

She looked at him with shock. "You're sorry?"

He buttoned his shirt and tucked it inside his trousers. "I can't do this."

She rose to a seated position and moved to the far corner of the sofa, covering her nakedness with her hands. "You don't want me?"

He shook his head. "Not like this."

Marks phone rang. He debated answering it until he saw it was Aiden. It wasn't smart to ignore the boss. He looked at the tears pooling in Poppy's eyes and knew it wasn't wise to ignore her either. He was stuck between a rock and a hard place. It was a no-win situation.

Aiden's name flashed on the screen again and he made a calculated decision. He'd get Aiden off the phone so he could explain things to Poppy. If he was her first, it should happen with wine and flowers and candles.

"What's up?" He answered the phone with more curtness than intended.

"Mrs. Brown called, she says she needs your services."

"Seriously? It's her damned cat on the roof again. Isn't the fire department supposed to take care of stuff like that?"

Poppy put on her bra and pulled on her T-shirt. Watching her cover her amazing body was a crime in itself. Never before had Mark wanted to murder an old woman and her cat.

"She asked for you, but I can go myself if you're busy. Just tell me what you've got going on, and I'll drop what I'm doing."

There was no way he could tell his boss that he wanted to give his girl her first orgasm. With a sigh, he said, "Tell Mrs. Brown I'll be over in a second." He hung up and turned to the beautiful woman in front of him. "God Poppy, I'm so sorry. This isn't what I wanted to happen."

She stood in front of him and tapped her finger on the loosened knot of his tie. "It's exactly what I wanted to happen." Her shoulders rolled forward. "Looks like we were on separate pages again." She let out a sigh. "I just thought you wanted—" She picked up her purse and moved swiftly to the front door.

"I do. I want it so bad. It's just the timing is all wrong. You deserve more."

She looked at him with sadness in her eyes. "Now you're sounding like my father."

She opened the door and walked out.

CHAPTER THIRTEEN

Poppy made it a few blocks before her tears made it impossible to see the road clearly. The last thing she needed to add to her life or her family's was a car accident. They had enough trouble, there was no need to borrow more.

She pulled off to the side of the road and wept. How stupid did she feel to wantonly expose herself to the man she loved only to have him tell her he didn't want her.

He wanted her just fine until she told him he'd be her first.

She slapped her palm to the steering wheel, which hurt like the dickens, but at least she felt something other than stupid. The pain in her palm was nothing compared to the ache that sat between her thighs. Not even a dose of rejection could quell that need.

Clouds rolled across the sky as she sat and pondered her dilemma. Had Mark really told her he didn't want her? Or had she turned his words into something else. She replayed them in her head.

"Your first?" And "Not like this."

Deep inside she knew he wasn't rejecting her. He'd

always moved with caution when it came to their friendship. Too much damn caution. He spent more time trying to do what he thought was right than actually doing what was right.

As she dried her tears and attempted to pull onto the highway, a crack of thunder sounded and a bolt of lightning hit so close that her truck shuddered.

"Dammit!" Storms freaked her out. Always had since she was a kid and she found a cow in the pasture that had been struck by lightning. It had been an awful sight to see since the poor thing hadn't died but had lain there and moaned in agony. Her father had pulled his pistol from his belt and put it out of its misery.

She put the truck in gear and gunned the engine. If she hurried, she could get home before the rain really let loose.

She got another block when the skies opened up and the torrential rain came down. The swish of her wiper blades took on a frantic pace, but the deluge was too much for them to handle. She inched forward in the seat like a granny with her chin perched over the steering wheel.

The nearly bald tires slid on the slick highway. She slowed it down to a crawl. It was just a few long blocks from the ranch. A mile or so to the turnoff and then another mile on the graveled road to home. She could make it.

Up ahead the road dipped. It no longer looked like a gully but a raging river as she neared it. Her only chance to get through it was to hit the gas and hope for the best.

"Here goes." She lead-footed it down one side of the hill and hit the running water at a speed that sent the old heap gliding across the surface. The only problem was she didn't float to the other side of the road.

The truck hydroplaned, turned, and went crashing off the side into a drainage ditch. The engine ran for seconds before it coughed, sputtered, and died. Being stranded in the drainage ditch was worse than on the road because all overflow rain was traveling down the washout. Every few seconds the car shuddered and moved a few feet down.

Another crack of lightning broke through the sky, and Poppy hunkered down. She slid so low she was almost sitting on the floor, and that's when she realized the runoff water had gotten so deep it was seeping into the truck and covering the floorboards.

"What now?" she yelled to the universe. She knew it wasn't smart to ask because, in her experience, the world wasn't kind. How could it be when it gave a ranching family five daughters not interested in ranching and only one son who was happy with the status quo. When the glue to her family sat broken in the living room? When the man she loved was too honorable and too good to take her virginity on the couch of his living room?

Lying on the front bench of the old truck, she curled into a ball and watched the water seep inside. Another boom of thunder. A bolt of lightning and a quick lurching of the truck sent her heart racing. She risked a peek outside to find herself floating down the ravine, picking up speed as the water rose.

Any normal person would pull their cell phone out and call for help, but she didn't have one. It was a luxury she couldn't afford. Hell, they still had a rotary dial phone hanging on the wall.

When she got out of this mess, if she got out of this mess, the first thing she promised to do was get a phone. The second thing was to march over to Mark's house and drag him to bed because there was no way she was dying a damn virgin.

As luck would have it, or her lack of luck, her truck hit

something solid. The force of the water was too great to keep her upright. She fell in what felt like slow motion as the heap of junk croaked and groaned before it flipped on its side.

Her mother used to tell her that life whispered messages. This was no whisper, it was bellowing at her to get the hell out of the truck.

Disoriented, she pushed her body off the steering wheel and searched for her purse. If she was going down, it wouldn't be without identification. With the strap hung over her shoulder, she moved toward the only exit and that was up. It took her three tries to force the door up and open. Took her another four to heave herself out of the space.

The truck was moving steadily toward the spillway, a drop-off that opened into the storm drains. She felt like a boat without a rudder.

The sky burst into light, which made her want to climb back into the cab of the pickup but seeing the drop-off approach gave her one shot. She ran across the side panel and hoped she'd clear the bank.

She hit hard, a stabbing pain shooting from her ankle to her knee. She thought maybe she'd broken something. As she slipped toward the water, she clawed at the grassy embankment, trying to gain purchase on anything. Her hand gripped an exposed root. If she couldn't pull herself up at least she could hold tight. Surely someone would come looking for her, wouldn't they? She prayed that Mark would, that somehow, he'd hear her and find her.

She didn't know if she could hold on any longer, and it had felt like an eternity although she didn't know how long she'd clung to the root. Just as her strength was giving out, she was lifted into the air by strong arms.

"What the hell, happened? Are you okay?" Mark pulled

her into his arms. "I'm so happy I found you." He looked downstream to where her truck had tipped over the edge of the spillway and landed with a crash.

Though she couldn't see it, she heard the way the metal collapsed from the fall. A shiver ran down her spine. She'd barely avoided her demise.

"I prayed that you'd find me." She was still in his arms but wiggling to be set free.

"Stay still, you could be hurt." He set her on the grassy knoll and began a thorough hands-on inspection. If she wasn't so tired, she might have enjoyed it.

"I am hurt. You pushed me away once you found out I was a virgin. What's the matter? You don't like innocents?"

Mark stopped and looked at her for the briefest of seconds.

"You? Innocent?" His hands moved over her face and touched a knot that was forming on her forehead. "You may be technically a virgin, but that mouth of yours...that damn mouth..." He moved his hand down her body. There was nothing sexual about it. Sitting in the frigid rain should have made her shake and shiver with cold but she was hot. Some from temper but most from passion. "I want you bad, Poppy. Being your first is going to be my pleasure, but I'm not taking you on my couch during a brief interlude."

She lifted on her elbows and watched him skim his hands over her legs, checking for broken bones. "You think it's going to be a pleasure?"

He touched her ankle and she winced.

"Baby, I'm going to love you like no other."

Despite the pain in her ankle, she laughed. "Not hard for you because there haven't been others."

He turned her ankle and while it was sore, it didn't appear to be broken.

He stood and cupped his erection, not hard to define since his clothes were soaked to his skin. "I'm always hard for you. Painfully hard. Don't think for a second that I didn't consider taking what I consider mine in my living room, but Poppy... Dammit, you deserve better and I'm not talking about a better man." He plopped onto the sodden ground beside her. "I'm the best man for you. All I'm saying is it should be special."

She crawled into his lap and laid her head on his chest. "It would have been. I was with you."

He groaned, deep in his throat. "You're killing me." He lifted her chin and looked into her eyes, but that didn't seem to be enough for him because he threaded his hand into her wet hair and pulled her head back, tilting her mouth to the perfect angle. Rain spattered in her face. She closed her eyes and surrendered to him completely. When the next boom of thunder and crack of lightning slit the air, she had no fear because if she died, she'd do it happily in Mark's arms.

He kissed her like they did in the movies. The kind of kiss lovers who'd been separated for years did. It was hungry and untamed. They had no concern about the rain. Neither cared that they were soaked to the bone. When his lips covered hers, a burning heat surged through her body. If she thought the space between her legs ached before, it was nothing to the sensation building there now. Not only did she ache with need but she was on fire from it.

His hand cupped her breast and she moaned.

Wiggling in his lap, she felt his baton, not the one he used for work, but the one he'd use on her when the time was right.

Her hand pressed against his chest. The pounding of his heart beat against her palm.

He pulled away. "You scared the shit out of me."

She rested her head on his shoulder and looked up at the water dripping from his beautiful, strong nose. "How did you find me?"

"Your father called the station looking for you. I knew you were heading home."

"Oh, God. Really? I'm almost thirty."

He chuckled. "You're only twenty-eight. Don't race ahead of yourself. Besides, you'll always be his little girl."

She shivered in the cold. "Sounds like you're on his side now."

He rose with her in his arms and started toward the road. "After you started talking about our children, I put myself in your father's shoes. He's not wrong to want to protect you."

"But he's wrong about you."

Mark held her tight as he worked his way toward the road, which was at least a half a mile away. "Yes, he is, but it's my job to show him the man I am."

"Will you do that for us?"

He stopped and looked at her with such sweetness. If she wasn't certain she'd die from hypothermia, she could have stayed right there forever. "I should have done it years ago. Deep inside, I wondered if your father was right. Am I my father's child?"

"No. I mean you're definitely his child, but you're not him. His sins are his, not yours."

He nodded as he made his way to the cruiser, which was parked on the side of the road.

"True, but all this time I could have been proving myself instead of staying clear. I thought I was doing what was best." He set her down next to the door.

Her ankle protested. "I think I sprained it."

He opened the door and helped her inside. "I know you did, it's swollen and turning purple. You really should see Doc Parker and get an X-ray."

"It's just a sprain." She rolled her ankle around to prove nothing was broken. "Take me home and I'll wrap it up."

He buckled her in and kissed her cold lips. "I'll take care of you. You're mine, Poppy, and I take care of what's mine." He rounded the cruiser and climbed inside. "You're also getting a cell phone. You could have died." He rubbed his face with his palm.

She nodded, knowing that was the truth. "How did you know I was here?"

He shrugged. "I don't know. I saw the water in the road and I knew. It was like you were calling to me. Asking me to find you."

She moved as far as her seatbelt would allow and leaned her head on his shoulder. "I did ask for you to find me. You came for me."

"I promise from now on, I'll always come for you, Poppy." He was about to kiss her when his police radio crackled.

"Mark, come in."

He picked up the handpiece. "I'm here, Coop. I've got her. She's bruised and wet but she's okay. Can you call her father and tell him we're on our way?"

CHAPTER FOURTEEN

Mark pulled the cruiser in front of the house and set the emergency brake. "Give me a minute to look at you." He reached forward and pulled a leaf from her hair. "You're a beautiful mess, Poppy Dawson. A damn beautiful mess."

A prickle of awareness skated over her skin. Goosebumps rose but it wasn't because she was soaked to the bone. It was because Mark was there. He'd come for her. He'd saved her.

She leaned forward to kiss him but he shook his head. That little shake of his head felt like a slap to her face.

"Don't you dare push me away again. I'm tired of your desert heat followed by your arctic freeze. Make up your mind about me."

He chuckled. "Maybe you hit your head too. Obviously, you don't remember me telling you that you were mine. I'm not fickle, Poppy. I won't change my mind or run hot or cold."

"Then kiss me."

He shook his head again. "We've got an audience." He nodded toward the porch, where her father stood leaning against the rail. His shotgun was propped against the wall. "I want to live long enough to have more than a kiss. I want it all."

"All of me?"

He licked his lips and smiled. "Every delicious inch of you. Someday, when you're ready, I'm going to show you pleasure like you've never known."

"I'm ready." She hardly recognized the breathy voice that came out of her mouth.

"There's no rush. We'll know when it's right." He waited until the windows fogged and leaned in to give her a quick kiss. "Let's get you inside so you can get dry."

Her lips tingled and her core vibrated with need—need that would never get satisfied living under her parents' roof.

He opened his door and disappeared into the rain only to show up to her side seconds later. She slid from her seat without putting too much pressure on her left foot.

Her father came down the steps to meet them halfway. "Where's the truck?"

Something inside her flared up as she limped toward the house. "I show up in a police cruiser, and limp toward the house, and all you care about is the damn truck." Her voice raised an octave from the first word to the last. "I'm hurt. I'm wet. I'm pissed." She stopped while the rain came down around them. "I hydroplaned and ended up in the drainage ditch. The water was so deep and moved so fast it took the truck to the spillway. I jumped out before it went over the edge." She turned into Mark's chest.

"Her ankle is sprained," Mark added. "I found her clinging to a root."

Lloyd looked between the two of them. "I'm sorry, are you okay?"

She looked at her father. "No. I'm not okay. I'm cold. I'm tired. I'm hurt and I'm hungry."

"You're also late." He scowled at Mark.

They moved to the porch to get out of the rain. "Yes, because Mark and I were at the sheriff's office doing it on the desk, Dad. The whole truck story and sprained ankle is just a cover-up."

Mark piped in. "She's kidding, sir, not about the truck but about, you know, the desk. I'd never—"

Poppy growled. "Never a truer statement. He'd never, which is why I'm the only twenty-eight-year-old virgin in Aspen Cove. Probably the whole damn state."

Her father smiled. "After hearing that, I don't even mind losing my truck." He laughed and walked into the house, leaving them on the porch.

"Poppy, do you think it's wise to bait your father?"

She hobbled over to the porch chair and flopped down. "No, but I'm tired of it all. I'm tired of fighting for everything."

He squatted in front of her. "Don't ever give up the fight. If it's worth having, it's worth fighting for."

The door opened and her sister Violet walked out. "Mom says to come on in. She wants Mark to join us for supper." She grabbed the door handle and stopped. "You really haven't done it?"

"Oh my God, you heard?"

Violet laughed. "I'm sure everyone within a five-mile radius heard."

Poppy eyed her sister. "At least I'm not alone."

Violet turned to Mark. "You too?"

Poppy gripped Mark's shoulders to help her stand. "I was talking about you."

A sly smile lifted Violet's lips. She shook her head.

"Stephen Castor, fellow camp counselor. Nothing to write home about."

Violet went inside and Poppy groaned. "I'm mortified. Even the damn chickens get more action than me, and there's only one rooster."

Mark pulled her to his chest and whispered into her hair. "Poppy, it's nothing to be ashamed of, in fact, I'm elated that I can be your first and last."

She frowned. "All talk and no action."

He moved them so they couldn't be seen. "When we're ready." He kissed her.

It wasn't a quick kiss like he gave her in the car. This kiss was full of promise and passion, and she wanted more, so much more.

"I'm ready."

"So, you keep telling me."

They made it into the house. Her mother was sitting in her wheelchair. "You okay?" she whispered.

Poppy smiled and walked toward her mother, trying not to limp. "Yes, I'm fine. The truck is gone but I'm good." She turned to her father, who was sitting in his lounger. "At least one parent was worried about me."

It was rare for her mother to smile, but her lips lifted into a grin. A big beautiful grin that made Poppy suck in a breath. Sometimes it happened organically, but it rarely happened any more with purpose. However, even Carol's eyes smiled.

Like any illness, there were good days and bad days. Lately, the bad outweighed the good but today was a great day. She was smiling and talking. Her skin had a pink glow to it.

Poppy wanted to smack her father upside the head. While her mother hadn't shown great improvement since

Doc, Lydia and Sage had been making daily house calls, she did look healthier. ALS wasn't something she'd ever recover from but she'd be able to hold on longer with proper medical care.

"Mark," Carol whispered. "Stay for dinner."

"Now, Carol," Lloyd said. "He's got stuff to do."

"He has to eat, Lloyd." As much as her voice would rise, this was Carol's yell. "The least we can do is feed the man since he saved Poppy's life."

"Come here, Mark."

He walked to her and lowered to his haunches in front of her. Poppy loved seeing him in their house. Loved that her mother respected Mark. Appreciated that her mother wasn't opposed to them dating.

"How's your mother?"

It surprised Poppy to hear her mother being so chatty. Generally, a few sentences were all she could get out before she was exhausted.

"She's good. She asked about you. Says she misses you." He went on to tell her that his mother was making all sorts of jams and jellies and selling them at farmer's markets and boutiques.

"That's wonderful," she responded. "Come closer."

He did and her mother whispered something in his ear. It was a secret between the two of them. When Mark stood up, he smiled. "I promise," was all he said.

"Get changed and get Mark a towel. In fact, get him one of your father's shirts so he can get dry too."

"Now, Carol—" Lloyd complained.

"Stop," she said.

Once out of sight, Poppy hobbled down the hallway. She came back ten minutes later to find Mark helping her brother and sister set the table. She handed him a plain black T-shirt.

He looked at it with skepticism. "It's mine." She rose on tiptoes until she could whisper in his ear. "I wear it to bed with nothing underneath."

She pushed it into his hands and directed him to the bathroom. When he returned, he was smiling. So was she because she loved the way her T-shirt stretched tightly across his chest. Despite it being a large, it hugged every one of his muscles.

In an event that she never thought she'd see, they all sat down to a family dinner. Her father sat at one end while her mother sat at the other. She couldn't eat the baked chicken Violet made every Sunday but she enjoyed chicken broth and conversation.

"I hear you murdered the truck," her brother said.

"Geez, people. How about 'I'm so glad you're all right.'"

Violet yanked a leg from the plate. "We are glad. It would be a shame for you to die a virgin."

Poppy turned to her father. "Permission to kill her now?" She picked up her knife and palmed it like a weapon.

"Put the knife down, Poppy, or I'll have to put you in cuffs."

She dropped the knife and smiled at him. "All talk and no action."

Her father's mouth dropped open as did her brother's, but her mother's body began to shake and out of nowhere came a laugh.

It took ten minutes for Carol to stop. Her body had taken control, and it had to run its course but the laugh was magical. Pretty soon everyone was chuckling. Including her father.

While the day had gone from good to bad, it ended as

the best day she'd had in a long time. Having Mark at the dinner table was a hell-freezes-over moment. It was proof that sometimes life had plans of its own.

After dinner, Mark helped clean up and they sat on the front porch while he wrapped her ankle with an elastic bandage.

"I'll pick you up for work on Friday."

"You'd do that for me?"

"Poppy, I'd do anything for you."

She narrowed her eyes. "You mean *almost* anything." She figured if she pressured him enough maybe they'd actually make it to the next phase of their relationship. They'd been at phase one for almost three decades. She needed fast-forward from this point on.

"I'll do that too, but it needs to be special. Not a quickie on the couch of my living room."

She had to give him credit. Most men would have taken what she offered. "You're right. They say you never forget your first."

His brow lifted. "You plan to have many after me?"

She giggled. "Depends. You promised me pleasure like I've never known. Can you deliver?"

He looked around as if afraid someone was watching. Poppy knew no one was. Both her father and brother would be glued to the television watching whatever sports were on. Violet would have her nose buried in a book. Her mom was already falling asleep before they stepped outside.

"Poppy," he whispered. "I'm going to do things to your body that will make you weep with joy. When my tongue tastes you, you will hate yourself for waiting so long, but I will love you even more because you waited for me. When I finally press myself inside you, you'll scream my name over and over again followed by the words *more* and *harder*."

Her heart raced. Who knew her Mark had such a naughty side. "Is there anyone local I should thank for your skills?" She hated to think of him with other women but good sex wasn't something a person learned on the internet. It was a skillset acquired by experience.

"Nope, you're the only girl for me in Aspen Cove."

She reached out and poked his chest. "I better be the only girl for you anywhere, buster."

He covered her mouth with his and she got lost in the kiss. If Mark made love with as much passion as he kissed, she would be one lucky girl.

CHAPTER FIFTEEN

Mark sat with the cruiser idling, waiting for Poppy to come out of the house. It had been two days since he'd seen or talked to her, but it didn't stop him from thinking about her. Hell, after their last conversation he'd taken three cold showers.

The door opened and out walked Lloyd. He looked at the cruiser and shook his head. After spitting into the bush by the stairs he walked toward the barn.

Lloyd Dawson confused him. How could a man who had once been so kind and caring turn into the curmudgeonly asshole he knew today? He remembered back when Lloyd used to joke around and play. He used to grow pumpkins for all the kids in town. In the fall, he'd hook the horses to a cart and have hayrides. Every year he held an autumn barn dance where the kids decorated their pumpkins and bobbed for apples.

Back then, Mark had been envious of the Dawson kids. They had it all. A big house, a lot of land, a father who adored them. That was until Mark's father stole everything.

He took their livelihood, took their trust, but most of all he'd taken Lloyd Dawson and changed him.

On some crazy level, Mark felt responsible for everything. There was nothing he could do to change anything. He couldn't have stopped his father from what he did. But he felt guilty by association. Lloyd held him responsible because he carried his father's DNA.

No amount of restitution would give this family back what they'd lost. How could you compensate a man for his loss of self-esteem?

The door opened again and Mark's heart lodged in his throat. Poppy Dawson was more than beautiful. When the sun caught her hair just right, she looked ethereal.

Today she wore a simple yellow dress with flat slip-on shoes. He was glad to see she no longer limped.

He hopped out of the car and raced to help her with her bag.

He gave her a quick kiss on her cheek. "Good morning, Poppy."

Every time she smiled, his stomach flipped and flopped. At thirty he thought he'd be over boyhood crushes but in truth, he'd never be over her.

"Good morning."

He helped her inside the car and rushed around to join her. On the seat between them, he had two things for her.

"I have your shirt." He held up the black T-shirt she'd let him borrow. "I was going to wash it, but then figured since it had touched my skin, maybe you'd want to wear it tonight." He licked his bottom lip. "Thought if you put it on your naked body, it might feel like we almost slept together." He would never tell her he slept in it for two days straight because it smelled like her.

She pulled it to her nose. "Have I told you how much I love your cologne?"

"You can tell me again." He knew how much she liked it. She commented all the time about how good he smelled. He'd recently picked up a new bottle of the expensive cologne just so he'd never run out.

"It makes me..." She blushed.

"Makes you what?"

She let out a low throaty chuckle. "Wet."

"Geez, Poppy, I swear you're going to kill me." He squirmed in his seat, feeling his trousers tighten. "You can't just blurt stuff like that out. I'm a mere mortal."

She turned to face him, the hem of her dress rising to show him the soft milky white of her thighs. "No double standards. You told me all the things you were going to do to my body the other day. What do you think that did to me?"

"Hopefully made you wet."

"You're impossible."

"Good thing you love me anyway." They hadn't actually exchanged the words. It was more like they moved around the emotion saying things like he just had. Was that fishing for the truth? Possibly, but when he told her he would make love to her, he meant it. It would be love for him. He knew she felt the same. It was in her green eyes; they lit up for no one but him.

"You're tolerable. I only keep you around because you smell good, and I need a ride."

Mark started the engine. Things were getting hot in the car and if he didn't get them moving, he wasn't sure they'd make it out of the driveway, but he was certain if he went with his instincts to take Poppy in his arms, Lloyd would definitely shoot him.

Before he put the cruiser in gear, he handed her the phone he'd purchased. "I never want you in a position where you can't call for help."

"You really bought me a phone?"

He shrugged. "It's a selfish gift because I want to be able to talk to you. Maybe we can say goodnight each night."

"It's my first."

He pulled around and headed back toward town.

"Looks like I'm going to give you a lot of firsts." Out of the corner of his eye, he saw a red flush rise to her cheeks.

"I've never had phone sex either."

He groaned. Today he'd have to take the long way around just so he wouldn't embarrass himself when he got out of the car.

"I swear, Poppy, after I make love to you, I'm going to swat that perfect ass for teasing me."

Joy swept through him when she squirmed in her seat. At least she was feeling it too.

When the town came into view, he reached over and held her hand. "Are you ready for our date tonight?"

She took a look at the bag by her feet. "Yep, you said to wear comfy clothes, closed-toe shoes and bring my camera."

"Good."

"Are you going to tell me where we're going?"

"Nope. Is your mom taken care of today? I don't want to take you someplace you can't be reached if she's not in good hands."

"We're going someplace remote?" She squeezed his hand. "You know if my dad catches us at one of his relief cabins, he'll be mad."

"We're not going to your father's hideaways."

Mark had forgotten about the cabins dotting the

Dawson property. To call them cabins was generous. They were a box with a bedroll at best. With unpredictable weather, there were several toward the outskirts of the Dawson land. Lloyd and his father had built them in case anyone working the lower or upper range would need a place to seek shelter if the weather turned.

"How do you know they're his hideaways?"

"You forget, I practically grew up on your range. Your dad had one he called his smoking cabin because your mom wouldn't let him smoke around the kids. My dad had one he called his drinking cabin. I'm pretty sure that cabin started all the problems. He spent a lot of his time there with a bottle."

She covered his hand with hers. "I'm so sorry all that happened but look at us now."

"We're figuring it out, aren't we?" He pulled into the spot in front of the sheriff's office.

"Yes, we are."

He rounded the car and helped her out. She reached for her bag, but he carried it for her. By the weight of it, he was certain she'd concealed a body. If he hadn't seen Lloyd walk to the barn, he might have considered it to be him.

"What's in this thing?"

"Since you wouldn't tell me where we're going, I wanted to be prepared for anything. I brought a few extra things like a bottle of wine and a box of condoms—a big box." She giggled as she headed for the door to the office.

"Poppy," he said in warning.

She turned. "Just kidding. I only brought three. I'm just a beginner."

She was through the door before he could say another word, but he still had her bag. He took it to his desk and unzipped it.

Inside there was a bottle of wine, two changes of clothes, and a book about photography. It was what weighed so damn much. Much to his relief—or disappointment—there weren't any condoms, but he couldn't comment because his boss was staring at him.

Mark walked the bag to Poppy's corner and tucked it next to the filing cabinet. "Just wait...I'll get you back."

"Good to see you both in one piece. I hear you had quite the swim the other day," Aiden said.

Poppy sat at her desk and organized her papers. "Not a swim really, but definitely a scare."

"Your knight in shining armor saved you."

"My knight in wet khakis definitely saved me but the old truck was a fatality, hence the knight bringing me to work in his trusty steed." She walked to Aiden and gave him a hug. "Thank you for letting Mark pick me up. I can't really afford to lose the hours."

Mark didn't like her hugging anyone but him.

Aiden patted her on the back and stepped away. "You think I let him? Mark told me, not asked me, but I would have said yes anyway." He walked to the coffeepot, where a half pot of day-old coffee sat warming.

The only time they drank fresh coffee was when Poppy was here or when Mark came on shift. That coffee was definitely yesterday's brew.

"Bobby came by earlier." Aiden took his seat. "He was able to pull what was left of your truck out of the spillway but said there isn't much to salvage. He asked if you wanted to sell it for scrap?"

"I figured as much. I'll go see him at lunch. How did he know where to find it?"

Aiden pointed to Mark. "Your knight."

"Speaking of knights, or in this case, nights"—Mark set

the new phone on her desk— "set this up so we can talk. It's attached to my account, so there aren't any restrictions."

Aiden rose. "Anyone want muffins?" He was out the door before they could answer. Katie always had a box waiting for them.

"I can't believe you bought me a phone." She opened the box and looked at it like he'd bought her a ring.

"I can't believe you don't have one yet."

"Not in the budget."

He understood. It all went back to his father. Once Mick Bancroft had hightailed it out of Colorado, Lloyd had reduced the number of cattle he raised since he could no longer trust the help. That reduction had put his family on a path to near poverty.

"Can you hold down the fort? I need to make sure my date arrangements are set."

"Do I get a hint?"

He thought about a way to get at her and it came to him. "Yes, I'll be tucked tightly between your thighs." He walked out and went straight to The Bait and Tackle Shop, which included outdoor sports equipment now that Bowie's friend Trig Whatley had come to town and partnered with him.

The bell above the door of the shop rang. He found Trig stocking lures. It was hard to believe he was missing a leg. Lost it in the war and claimed that he was alive because Bowie saved him. That might have been the first time he'd faced death, but last Christmas he'd gotten a wicked infection and almost died again. That time it had been a team effort with Dr. Covington, Doc Parker, and Sage being miracle workers, and Doc's daughter Charlie being too stubborn and in love to let him die.

"How's the wife?" It hadn't taken them long to tie the knot and start making babies. Two at once was the plan.

Not the original plan, but it was what was happening with Charlie pregnant with twins.

"She's finer than frog hair split seven ways. She's been home working on the nursery." Trig stood tall and proud. He walked behind the counter and took out a map and a set of keys to the four-wheeler Mark had rented. "I got what you needed." Once he opened the map, he pointed at the trail. "If you head up Old Camp Road, you'll reach the vista overlook. I took some hikers up there a couple of weeks ago and it's amazing."

"May have gone up there as a kid, but I don't remember."

Trig shook his head. "You'd remember. It's like you're sitting on top of the world. On a clear day, you can see Denver. You can even see Fury. Off to the right, if you look hard enough, you'll see the old Blackwood Mine. Everything is in bloom and sunset is gorgeous. Just be careful coming back down, and bring your gun in case you run into aggressive wildlife. That forestry guy has been tracking a wolf pack and a cougar."

"Kyle Morello is back?" He didn't know much about the man but had met his wife at B's Bed and Breakfast. Rumor had it they were like fire and ice when they met, but somehow it had all worked out.

"Nah, he was passing through a few weeks ago and stopped in to say hello. You need anything else?"

Mark thought of a lot of things he needed but none that Trig could offer. "Nope, off to make sure Maisey has her part of my plan in the works."

When he entered the diner, he found Maisey on the phone. She held up a finger to signal she'd be with him in a minute.

"Riley Black." Maisey raised her voice. "Don't you

argue with your aunt. You will come to Aspen Cove. Dalton already set aside a studio for you at the Guild Center, and Katie has agreed to rent you the apartment she has above the bakery."

Mark pointed to the coffeepot and waited for Maisey's nod of approval. Once it came, he poured himself a to-go cup of freshly brewed coffee.

"You worry too much. You've got a job at the diner." Maisey pointed at the phone and rolled her eyes while she mouthed the word *kids*. "I'll teach you everything. Meg is your age and works here full time. She can help you get settled. Just get in your car and come...I love you too, sweetheart." She hung up.

"Problems?" Mark asked.

"You know family, there's some you love and some you tolerate. My sweet little niece Riley has reached her saturation point. She needs a break from her immediate family."

That's how Aspen Cove was growing, one person at a time. "If she's like everyone else, she'll love it here."

"Got to get her here first. Loyalty always tugs at the heartstrings doesn't it?" She wiped her hands on her apron. "I bet you're here to make sure we don't forget your picnic basket."

He nodded. "Yep, just want our first real date to be special."

Maisey wrapped her arm in his and led him to the door. "It will be perfect. You leave it to me. I've known that girl since she was knee-high to a grasshopper. I've got you covered."

His last stop was the corner store where the owners, Phillip and Marge, had promised to bring in a fresh batch of flowers. With all the new couples in town, Mark was certain they sold more blooms than bread.

Confident he'd thought of everything, he went back to the office only to find out Mrs. Brown's cat was back on the roof.

CHAPTER SIXTEEN

Poppy watched the clock like somehow it would make the day go faster. It didn't.

After Mark left to run some errands, she set up her phone. It was such an adult thing to have. Even her sisters who were away at college didn't have cell phones. They borrowed friends' or used the payphone on campus.

She was about to make her first call to Mark when the desk phone rang.

"Sheriff's Department, Poppy speaking, how can I help you?"

"Send Mark now, please. Piddles is on the roof again."

Poppy felt bad that Mark was the one who was called time and again for Mrs. Brown's cat problems.

"You know, Mrs. Brown, when Piddles gets hungry, he'll come back inside." It wasn't that Mrs. Brown even cared about her darn cat being on the roof. It was that she liked to chat with Mark, who was too kind to shut her up and leave. It didn't hurt that he was easy on the eyes. Mrs. Brown was old, she wasn't dead. "You might consider closing the dormer window so Piddles can't get out."

"You might consider doing what I ask."

"Yes, ma'am. I'll let him know."

That window was the cat's only escape. If not a getaway from Mrs. Brown, then from having the name Piddles for a few glorious moments. She giggled to herself, giving the cat a voice and envisioning him standing on the rooftop with the wind in his fur and a Roman cape at his back meowing, "I am Sparticat."

Just as she was about to send her first text to Mark about the cat, he walked in.

"You have a pussy problem."

He stopped dead in the center of the room.

"I have a what?"

"I said you have a pussycat problem. Piddles is on the run again."

Mark groaned. "That is not what you said." He narrowed his eyes at her but his lip twitched. He was trying to hold back his smile but he couldn't quite do it.

"That is exactly what I said, you just heard what you wanted to hear," she teased. Her plan was to get him so worked up he couldn't help but take her home and make love to her.

"You're playing with fire here, Poppy. Don't push me." He stalked toward her.

She stood up and faced him with defiance. "Or what? You going to lock me in the cell? Cuff my hands to the bars and—"

In walked Aiden with a box of muffins in one hand and his daughter Kellyn in the other. "The boss is here, you better get to work," Aiden said, but he wasn't referring to himself. The new boss was Kellyn, but she ruled with a smile and a box of crayons.

"No problem, Mark was just on his way out to take care of a pussy...cat problem."

Aiden rolled his eyes. "Piddles again?"

"Yep." Mark pointed at Poppy. "We're not finished."

She laughed. "Far from it, mister."

The rest of the afternoon was spent filing paperwork and sending Mark text messages.

I've never met Piddles. Is he longhaired or neat and trimmed? How do you like your pussies?

Seconds later he responded.

I don't discriminate. As for Piddles, he's a Sphynx. Soft, smooth and warm to the touch. You know you're in trouble, right? If I fall off the roof because I can't walk with the pole between my legs, it's all your fault.

Poppy knew Mark wasn't still on the roof because Mrs. Brown had called to thank Aiden for having such nice employees. Well, everyone but that snarky little Poppy girl.

A tug on the skirt of her dress brought her out of her daydream.

"Wook, Poppy, I drew you a picture." Kellyn handed her a crayon drawing of a bride and groom.

"Is that your mom and dad?"

"No, silly. It's you and Mark."

Poppy pulled it to her chest. "That's the best picture I've ever seen. You're going to grow up to be an artist."

Kellyn shook her head. "Nope." She pointed down to the star on her chest. The one Aiden had made for her that said Kellyn Cooper Deputy in Training. "I'm going to be the next sheriff, and I'll give haircuts on Mondays."

Poppy couldn't help but laugh. Kellyn Cooper was

proof that love could conquer anything. Her mother had escaped an abusive husband, taking Kellyn with her. At the time, poor Kellyn had suffered such severe PTSD that she hadn't spoken a word and now she chattered on and on to anyone who would listen.

"I love that you want to be a hybrid law woman and hairdresser. It's good to keep your options open," Poppy said. She looked at Aiden, who had a look of pure adoration. His wife Marina was his moon and stars, but Kellyn was his ray of sunshine. Poppy wanted what they had. She wanted a family of her own.

"She's got you married off already," Aiden commented.

"It's my first wedding photo. I'm going to frame it." She traced the red-haired girl in the picture and leaned down so she was eye level with Kellyn. "You made me look so pretty." She moved her fingers to the dress. "I got married in yellow?"

Kellyn frowned. "The white wouldn't show up on the paper."

"I love it." She kissed the top of her head and tucked the picture into her drawer so she could take it home. She really did love it. More so because even a five-year-old could see that she and Mark were in love.

When Mark returned from his rounds that afternoon, he disappeared into the bathroom and came out wearing jeans and a snug, nothing-left-to-imagine T-shirt. Poppy didn't need to go anywhere on the date. She was happy to sit at her desk and stare at him.

"Aiden said we could leave early. Get changed and meet me out back. All you need is your camera and a light jacket."

She didn't need any other motivation. She grabbed her bag and ran for the bathroom. Five minutes later, she'd locked up the office and was standing behind the building alone. Movement ahead drew her attention to a four-wheeler. The man driving it was gorgeous.

"This is your chariot?"

He killed the engine, which was too loud to hear above.

"Chariot? This is your steed." He pointed to the label. "It says right here it has horsepower."

Strapped to the back was a picnic basket with a bouquet of flowers bungee-corded to the top.

"Are those for me?"

He looked over his shoulder. "No, they're for Mrs. Brown. You know how much I love her pus—"

Poppy gave him a light punch to the arm. "Don't you say it."

His full belly laugh filled the air. "Get on, sweetheart. Spread those thighs and cradle my hips between them."

She climbed on the back of the bike, tucking her camera and shoulder bag to the side of her body. "Is this what you had in mind when you said you would be between my thighs?"

"No, but it will have to do for now. Hold on tight."

She wrapped her arms around him and pressed her cheek to his back. He pressed the start button and they were off.

It took them an hour to reach a vista, where Mark set up a blanket and the basket.

"Alone at last." He patted the space beside him and Poppy joined him. They were at the edge of a cliff. The earth fell away only feet from them. The sky burst into flames of orange and yellow and red. Hints of blue and purple remained as the sun began its descent.

"So beautiful." She picked up her camera and took no less than a dozen shots.

"Yes, you are." He took the bottle of wine Poppy had brought and uncorked it. Inside the basket, Maisey had packed wineglasses and sparkling apple cider. Mark would stick with the cider but Poppy needed to unwind and relax.

She turned the lens to Mark. "I can't take enough pictures of you."

He poured her a glass of wine and offered it to her. "How many do you have?"

She took a sip and laughed. "You don't want to know."

"A lot?" He popped the top on the cider and filled a glass.

"Thousands."

"Probably an exaggeration."

"An under-exaggeration. You've been an unhealthy obsession for me for decades."

He tapped his glass to hers. "Cheers to obsessions. You've been mine."

They enjoyed a supper of fried chicken and biscuits, and when they were finished, they lay back on the blanket with Poppy's head on his chest. The first stars of the night were starting to twinkle in the twilight.

"Are we safe up here for a while?" She snuggled closer.

He pulled his gun from his belt and put it on the blanket next to them. "Outside of a few hungry wolves and a rogue cougar, I think we'll be okay."

She stiffened. "Oh my God, I don't want to get eaten on our first date."

He moved from beneath her to above her. His hair caught the last of the day's light, casting an almost blue shadow across the sweep of his bangs.

His hands went to the button of her jeans. "Are you sure about that?"

CHAPTER SEVENTEEN

This wasn't part of the plan, but Poppy would never know how much she tortured him until he showed her what she was missing. While it was about teaching her a lesson, it was also about teaching her the pleasures he could bring her.

With a tug, he popped the button of her jeans free.

"What are you going to do?" she asked. Her words were quick and breathy.

"Oh, you'll see." In the fading light of the day she lay there with remnants of the sky's orange glow warming the paleness of her skin. He moved her zipper down a tooth at a time, giving her the chance to say no. "You want me to stop?"

"How can I want you to stop when I don't know what I'm in for?"

With her pants unbuttoned and unzipped, he moved down her legs to her shoes. "You don't need these." He eased them off and set them aside, then moved back to the waistband of her jeans. "Or these." He cleared her hips and sucked in a breath when he saw the pink lace panties she wore. It was a stretch to call them underwear when they were no bigger than a Band-Aid and floss.

"No sphinx here." She moved her hands to cover the tiny strip of fabric and neatly trimmed patch of hair.

"I'm glad." He moved her hand away to take in her loveliness. "Don't hide from me. I've been waiting years to see you." He thumbed the fabric on each side and eased it down with the help of her lifting her hips.

She closed her eyes.

"Open your eyes, Poppy. I know you're hiding, but I see you, and what I see is beautiful." He straddled her hips and lowered his lips to hers. "You still okay with this?" He gave her a long languid kiss. Her mouth opened and his tongue slid inside. She always tasted so sweet. His mouth watered, knowing he'd get a full helping of her soon.

"Yes, I'm ready for whatever this is." She reached for his belt. Though his hard-on pressed painfully against his pants, this was about her. Pleasing her would please him.

He palmed her hand. "Not tonight. This is about you."

She shook her head. "It's about us."

"Yes, it is, but what I'm going to do is about you." He stopped any rebuttal with a swift bite to her lower lip and a long sensuous kiss that had her hips circling beneath him. He rose and gripped the hem of her shirt, and with one swift pull, she was almost naked. Under the light of the rising moon, she glowed like an angel. "You don't need this either." Reaching behind her he unfastened her bra and pulled it away. "Do you have any idea how stunning you are?" He shifted his legs to nudge hers open. Leaning back on his heels, he took her in. Where was her camera when he needed it?

"I feel funny being the only one naked. At least take off your shirt."

He crossed his arms, grabbed the hem and pulled it free. While she caressed his chest, he did the same to hers. With each brush of his thumb, the tiny buds turned into pebbles. It didn't take much stroking and caressing to make her moan.

"Oh, my God, I've truly been missing out."

"You have no idea, but we're going to make up for lost time." He bent over and pulled a nipple into his mouth. Her hips shot off the ground. He moved to the other with the same result. His Poppy was going to be a firecracker in bed.

Leaving her panting, he moved south, tickling her stomach, nibbling on her hips and hovering over her sex, his hot breath driving her nuts. "You remember what I told you I would do to you?"

She lifted on her elbows to see him settling himself between her open legs. "You said you'd get me back. Is this where you get me all hot and bothered and then tell me to pack up so we can go home?"

"No." He shook his head but wasn't sure she could actually see him. "This is where I taste you and make you wonder why you waited so long. But when I'm finished for the night, you'll be glad you did."

She didn't have a chance to think about his words. His tongue ran the length of her.

"Oh, my God," she cried out. She tried to squirm away. Mark knew it wasn't because she actually wanted to escape, but because the pleasure was too intense and they were just getting started.

"You taste amazing." He licked and laved at her until her body shook, and he pulled back until she calmed. Each time he took her to the edge and retreated, she threatened to do bad things to him. He had no idea what she had in mind, but bad things with Poppy sounded good.

"This is you getting me back, isn't it?" The words escaped choppy and throaty.

"You bet your ass." He covered her sex once again, but this time he pulled the tight little bundle of nerves into his mouth and sucked until she exploded. When the arch of her back met the ground and tense thighs relaxed, he started in on round two.

"That feels so good and bad. It almost hurts but doesn't."

He lifted his lips and smiled. "Tomorrow and every other day you see me, you're going to look at me and smile. Each time I lick my lips or put on Chapstick, you'll know that I'm thinking about this moment and how you taste and how amazing it feels to make you quiver against my lips. You'll never forget that these lips made you come with such ferocity, your entire body participated from the tingling of your hair to the curling of your toes. I will be your first and your last, Poppy, because no one can love you like I do."

It didn't take him long to put her over the edge again. Only this time, she wasn't screaming for God, she was screaming for Mark, and his name rolling off her lips in the middle of an orgasm was all he needed.

Well, not all he needed. He would be taking a cold shower when he got home.

When he was finished, he dressed her, then himself, and pulled her back into his arms. They lay on their backs and watched the stars.

"You okay, Poppy?" He stroked her hair and down her back.

"Mmm-hmm, I'm perfect."

"You are."

In the mountains, without the saturation of city lights, there were a million stars in the sky. It wasn't odd to see a few shooting from one edge to the other. When the first ball of light glided over them, Poppy told him to make a wish.

He closed his eyes and asked for the next fifty years of their lives to be easier than the last twenty. There was no doubt they would still face obstacles, but at least Lloyd wasn't verbally threatening to shoot him anymore. He kept his gun on the porch as a visual reminder. Mark had no idea what the death of Poppy's mom would do to them. He was bracing himself for hard times. As far as he knew, his father was still alive but when he left the family, it had been felt almost like a death. That was bad enough for him. He couldn't imagine what the real deal would feel like.

"I forgot to ask if you checked in with your mom before we left."

She nodded against his chest. "Yes, she was good. Sage had been by the house. Katie brought little Sahara over because my mom loves to see how fast she's growing. When I work, Violet stays with her. I think she might have a little crush on fireman Luke, though she knows he's way too old for her."

Mark laughed. "Yes, he is. He's like twice her age."

"You sound like a big brother ready to defend her honor."

"You're her sister, I'm your boyfriend, that makes her an honorary sister. Besides I'm not a fan of Luke Mosier after you and he tried to make me jealous."

It was her turn to laugh. The sweet sound filled the air, mixing with the chirps of crickets and the slight wind rustling the leaves of the trees.

"It worked, right? If he hadn't made you jealous, you wouldn't have kissed me in the street, confronted my father, or taken me up here to do wicked things to my body."

"You liked those wicked things."

She pulled her jacket tighter and leaned into him to soak up his warmth. "I did. I think I'll be feeling the burn of your whiskers for a while."

"Good, it will remind you who you belong to, and it's not Luke Mosier."

"It's always been you, Mark. Always you."

He hadn't planned on saying the exact three words yet either. It seemed too quick, but in reality, they'd been attached at their souls since they were kids.

He picked her up and set her in his lap so they were face to face—her legs straddling his. He cupped her cheek and brought his lips a whisper away from hers.

"I love you, Poppy Dawson. I always have, and I always will. My heart belongs to you."

A single tear ran down her cheek. "I love you, Mark Bancroft. I always have, and I always will. My heart and my body belong to you."

She leaned forward and gave him a kiss that reminded him why they needed to pack up and leave. He needed that cold shower.

He lifted her to her feet and packed up their basket. She looked inside and saw her favorite cherry pie. "Maisey packed dessert. We never ate it."

He hugged her tight and whispered in her ear. "I had dessert, that's for you." He knew if he could see her face, she'd be cherry-pie red. "Mine was sweet and satisfying."

"When will I get your body?"

He tied the basket to the back of the four-wheeler and climbed on, patting the seat behind him so she'd hop on.

"Soon. When we're ready."

She slid behind him and hugged him tight. "Lots of promises and no action," she teased.

"Poppy, our next date is all about the action. Friday too soon?"

Her body shivered. "Friday sounds amazing."

"Sweetheart, you have no idea how amazing it's going to be."

CHAPTER EIGHTEEN

Friday morning, Poppy got up early to get her chores out of the way. Mark was picking her up for work and since they had a date tonight, she wouldn't have much time to help around the ranch after her shift.

She fed the horses, collected eggs, and was mucking stalls when her father arrived.

"Why you up so early?"

Poppy wanted to roll her eyes. It wasn't like she hadn't been pulling Friday shifts at the sheriff's office for months. "I've got work."

He frowned. "I'm tired of that boy coming around here all the time. I don't like him, Poppy."

She tossed the rake against the wall. "Unless you want me to take the tractor, my horse or your truck to work, you'll have to put up with him coming around." She stood in front of her father and fisted her hips. "In fact, you should be thanking him for taking the time to get me, otherwise you'd have to drive me."

"I don't like it." He grabbed another rake and moved clean hay into the already emptied stalls.

"You don't have to, but you have to deal with it. And stop calling him *that boy*. Mark is a man. He's thirty years old, and I like him enough for both of us."

"Is this your early shift?"

Him asking meant he knew exactly what days she worked, and two Fridays a month she worked until noon. Today was her early shift.

"Yes, but I'm staying in town for a while."

"Seeing that bo...man."

She let out a growl. "His name is Mark, which you know because you've been terrorizing and tormenting him since he was eight." She watched his lips thin to a mere crack on his face. "Wasn't it you who burned down Grandpa's barn when you were sixteen?"

"That was different. I was wooing your mother and set up candles that we happened to knock over when we were..." He coughed. "Never mind. It was different."

"You're right. It was different because you were sixteen and knew better. Grandpa could have told you to get lost. Forbid you to marry his daughter. He could have judged you by your own stupidity, and it would have been fair." She picked up a shovel and took her frustration out on the pile of horse dung that needed to be moved outside. "You, on the other hand, never judged Mark by his own actions. You judged him by his father's, which had nothing to do with him."

Her father stood up and leaned on the handle of the rake. "What do you want me to do?"

"I want you to get over it. I'm in love with him and because of his respect for you, he's stayed away. But no more, we are moving fast forward on our relationship. We've wasted ten years. I can't please two men in opposition. Don't make me choose, Dad, I'm not sure you'd come out on top this time."

She swallowed the lump in her throat. She'd been asserting her independence lately, but never had she been so honest.

"You live in my house and you'll live by my rules. Don't forget that."

"If it weren't for Mom, I'd be long gone. She's the reasonable one. You're...you're just a bitter man who's lost everything once and gave up the rest along the way."

"I won't let you disrespect me. Nor will I ever allow him to be a part of our family. You may have to choose. Choose wisely." Her father threw down the rake and walked toward the door.

When Poppy looked up, she saw Mark standing there. Concern was written all over his face. He moved forward and pulled her into his arms. "You okay?"

No. "Yes, I'll be fine." It was a lie she'd told herself the past several years. Years when all her high school friends were getting married and having children. While she mucked out the stalls and rode the fences, they were decorating nurseries and celebrating marriage milestones.

She was never one to have pity parties. She didn't have the luxury of being self-indulgent. Her life was on autopilot. It wasn't until that kiss in the street that she realized she could have more. Deserved more.

With her arms wrapped around Mark's waist, she shook. Sobs racked her body. Tears streamed down her face. All the while, he held her. Kissed the top of her head and promised everything would be all right, but she wasn't so sure.

When she calmed down. He guided her to a bale of hay and asked her to sit. He stripped off his uniform shirt, which left him in a plain white T-shirt, and he finished her morning chores.

After he was done, he stood in front of her. "Go get your stuff, and I'll be waiting in the cruiser."

"I'm a mess. I need a shower."

He lifted his nose in the air. "You smell amazing." He sniffed his T-shirt. "That's me you're smelling."

She stood and buried her face into the center of his chest. "I love you. Thanks for being here at the perfect moment."

His somber expression concerned her. "I heard some of your conversation with your father."

"How much?"

"Enough to know I don't want you to have to choose. That never works out for anyone."

Tears welled up in her eyes despite all the crying she'd done earlier. "I don't want to have to choose either, but if I had to choose, I'd choose you." She walked toward the door. "I've chosen him for the last ten years, and see where it's got me?"

Mark grabbed his shirt from the hay bale and wrapped his arm around her shoulders. When they got back to the house, Doc was just leaving.

Poppy rushed ahead. "Everything okay?" Doc didn't always have a smile on his face, but he rarely had a frown.

"Your mom's struggling a bit today. I upped her oxygen levels. We'll see what happens."

"Should she go to the hospital?"

Doc shook his head. "I tried, but that's not what she wants."

Poppy fisted her palms. "You mean it's not what my father wants."

Doc set his hands on her shoulders. "No, your mother

said no hospitals, and I have to honor her wishes. When she got sick, she made out an advance medical directive. No hospitals, she has a DNR. This is all about her, Poppy. Not about what you think your father wants. He's been trying to get her into long-term care for months."

Poppy stumbled back. She had no idea. "Are you sure?"

He nodded and walked to his car. "If I'm right, you've got an appointment today, correct?"

"Yes, I'll see you then."

Mark, who'd been standing silently beside her, asked, "Are you sick?"

"No, it's girl stuff."

His eyes got that deer-in-the-headlights look. "Oh."

"If we're going to be intimate, I need birth control."

His shocked expression turned into a smile. "Right." He nodded like a bobble doll. "Do you want to wait until they take effect?"

She laughed. "No, haven't we waited long enough?"

He slipped on his shirt and started to button it. "Yes—yes, we have."

She slid her hands up his chest and helped him. "Glad we're on the same page." She looked over her shoulder toward the door. "Give me ten minutes to shower and change." She gave him a quick kiss and disappeared. "You can stay here or come inside and visit my mother."

He seemed to debate the two but followed her inside the house.

Poppy did her best to get ready in ten minutes but it took her fifteen, and when she came downstairs, she found Mark sitting next to her mom, holding her hand.

Mom's voice was a whisper at best but Mark leaned in with his ear next to her lips and listened to every word she said.

Violet stood in the kitchen, leaning against the counter. "They kicked me out."

Poppy looked back into the living room and watched Mark nod. She barely picked up the words when he said, "I will, that's a promise."

When he stood, he had a look of calm about him. "You ready?"

Poppy hugged Violet. "Doc says she's struggling today. Call me if she needs anything. If you need anything."

Violet glanced at Mark. "I need a boyfriend."

"We'll work on that," Poppy responded

Mark held out his hand and led her to the cruiser.

"Maybe I should stay with her today."

He chuckled. "Your mom said you'd say that and she made me promise to take you to work."

"Was that the promise I heard?"

"One of them. Your mom is very demanding. She wants what's best for all of you."

Mark turned the car toward town, then reached over and held Poppy's hand. "You smell great."

She sniffed the air. "You still stink."

He laughed all the way to the sheriff's station.

AFTER POPPY FINISHED HER SHIFT, she walked over to the clinic to visit Dr. Lydia Covington.

"What were you thinking for birth control?" Lydia asked.

Poppy had done a lot of investigating the past few days. She wanted something effective but easily reversible. She hadn't been lying when she told her father she was on fast forward. At twenty-eight she was nearing the end of her prime fertility years. She'd read somewhere that after thirty, the quality of her eggs would slip.

"I was thinking about the pill?"

"Is there a reason?"

"Seems like the most common."

Lydia nodded. She explained the pros and cons to several forms of birth control, including condoms. Then she looked at Poppy's record. "How many sexual partners have you had?"

Poppy blushed. "None."

Lydia tried to hide her surprise, but the big eyes gave it away. "Did you say none?"

She hoped she wasn't in for another birds-and-bees conversation. "I'm waiting for the one."

Lydia patted her back. "Good for you."

After a thorough examination, Poppy left with a sample pack, a prescription and a box of condoms shoved inside her purse.

Mark was waiting outside for her. "Got everything you needed?"

She bit her lower lip. "Yep, now all I need is the action you promised."

He helped her inside the car and drove her home. "I'll pick you up at six."

The butterflies swirled in her tummy. Tonight was the night. Something told her that everything would change.

CHAPTER NINETEEN

Preparing for someone's first time was a big responsibility. The pressure to make it perfect was overwhelming. Mark left work early to set the night in motion.

First thing on his list was a talk with Cannon, who was his best friend. After hearing Lloyd tell his daughter he'd never be allowed to be part of their family, he was torn between what he wanted and what was right. He wanted Poppy, but he didn't want her to have to choose.

"Off early?" Cannon pointed to the cat clock on the wall. Its tail swished back and forth much like Mike, his one-eyed cat, who currently sat on the register with his tail mimicking the clock.

"Got a date with Poppy but I needed some advice."

"Condoms," Cannon blurted.

"No...I mean..." He let out a long sigh. "I'm not talking about our sex life with you."

"So, you have one. Good to know."

Mark shook his head. "Shut up and let me explain." He filled Cannon in on the conversation he'd overheard and Poppy's decision to choose him.

"I don't see what the problem is. She's got things squared away in her head."

"The problem is, that's her family and they hate me."

Cannon poured a short beer and set it in front of Mark. "I'm gonna tell you the same thing Doc told me when I was dealing with my drunken father."

"Oh no, if it's a Doc story, I may need a pint and honestly I don't have the time."

Cannon chuckled. He leaned against the back counter, facing the empty bar that would be full within the hour. "Now, son..."

Mark groaned because if Doc was giving a lesson he always started with "Now, son," and he thought it funny that Cannon did the same.

Cannon continued. "At some point, you make your own family. If people didn't move on from their parents, no one would have populated the world. Or everyone would be inbred with three eyes and two noses. Decide on who you want in your family and make it happen. DNA doesn't make a family. Love does." Cannon put one hand over his stomach and took a bow.

Mark had to admit that with age came wisdom, and Doc was right. Family started somewhere, and his would start with Poppy.

He thanked his friend, tossed back his drink for courage, and left for home.

It took him the rest of the afternoon to get things ready. He stopped by Dalton's and picked up a take-and-bake dinner with fresh vegetables and citrus chicken. As it cooked, he cleaned, organized and decorated for romance with flowers, candles, and wine.

The scene was set. All he needed was his date. After he showered, he left to get Poppy. Funny as it seemed, the closer he got, the more nervous he was. His palms sweated, his heart raced. What if somehow he messed up? What if, after all these years, they made love and it wasn't enough for her? He shook the crazy thoughts from his head. He was a good lover. A considerate lover, and he'd love on Poppy until he knew she was satisfied. The first encounter had been positive so why would this time be much different. *Because after tonight you'll have nothing left to give.* That was the issue. Once they'd made love, all his cards would be on the table.

This time when he pulled in front of the house, Lloyd wasn't standing on the porch and his shotgun wasn't leaning against the wall.

Mark knocked softly in case Carol was sleeping. Violet answered the door and nodded toward Poppy, who was squatting in front of her mother.

"I'm not leaving you."

He could hear the wheeze of the oxygen tank. Carol's skin was sallow with a blue tint.

Poppy turned around and the look of worry dulled her usually bright eyes. "We can't go."

Mark walked to her and nodded. "That's fine, sweetheart. We'll stay here." He'd have to go home to turn off the oven he had on warm but he would return and sit with Poppy and her mother all night if that's what she wanted.

Carols eyes widened, she took in a deep shaky breath. "No," she exhaled. "You. Go. Now."

"Mom, you're not sounding great."

Carol's eyes moved to Mark. "You promised."

His heart sank. Just that morning she'd made him promise to take Poppy out and have a good time. She told him to marry her daughter and make her happy. Give her babies and a reason to live and love.

"I did," he said. He turned to Poppy. "Don't make me break my promise to your mother. She wants us to go out and have a good time."

Poppy frowned. "I'm worried."

"Go."

He hadn't heard Carol speak so clearly.

"Go for me. Love won't wait." There was no room for doubt in her voice. She wanted Poppy and him together. She'd told him that much earlier, which eased some of the anxiety of dealing with her father. He had Carol in his corner, but she wouldn't be there long.

Poppy stood. "Mom, I love you."

Mark knew if Carol could move, she would have taken Poppy in her arms and hugged her. "I love you too," she said and closed her eyes.

Violet walked over. "Go have fun. She'll sleep the rest of the night, anyway. I heard her, she wants you to go."

Poppy swiped the tear from her cheek and nodded. "Okay. I'll go, but you have my cell number. Call me if something happens." She picked up her purse and laced her fingers through Mark's. They walked out the door hand in hand.

Poppy fretted the whole drive to his house.

"We can go back," he told her

"No. She wants this. Selfishly, I want this. I want you."

"It's not selfish to want what's yours."

He parked and walked her into the house. It smelled of savory chicken.

"Wow, the house looks amazing."

He took her coat and purse and led her to the table, where he lit the candles and poured her a glass of white wine.

"You want help?"

143

He shook his head. "No, I've got this."

He served up dinner and sat beside her. When he lifted his wineglass, he toasted. "Here's to us. Here's to a lifetime of love and lovemaking. Here's to a beautiful future. I love you."

"That was so sweet." The twinkle of sassiness was back in her eyes. "You know I'm a sure thing tonight. You didn't have to go through so much trouble to get me into your bed."

"You are worth this and so much more. Eat up. I don't want you worn out before we get started."

They enjoyed a leisurely dinner, another glass of wine and several hot and steamy kisses. Mark stood and offered her his hand. "Are you ready for more?"

She nodded. "I'm ready for everything."

He hoped so because he wanted it all too. She followed him into his room. It was dark until he lit the candles. The candlelight danced across the gray walls.

Everything was silent except her breath, which seemed to grow faster with each inhale and exhale.

"It's okay." He held both of her hands and gently walked her to the bed. "I'll take care of you."

"I know. It's just that I feel like I'm on a cliff, getting ready to jump. My heart is beating so fast."

"I'll catch you, Poppy. I'll always catch you."

He looked down at her. She might have been twenty-eight, but the innocence in her eyes made her look like a teen. However, her dress was all woman with its low-cut neckline and cinched waist. And those legs made him hard just imagining them wrapped around his waist, but he reminded himself that he had to take it slow.

He dropped to his knees and put his hands on her thighs. The cotton of her dress was so soft under his palms.

He reached up and started on the buttons that ran from the plunging neckline to the hem.

"Did you enjoy the other night?"

She ran her fingers through his hair. "You know I did."

He smiled at her and nipped at her lower lip as he continued to unbutton her dress. "I'm thinking that might be the way to start."

She shivered as her dress fell from her shoulders to the bedspread. With a shift of her hips, he pulled it free and set it aside.

Poppy sat on his navy blue spread dressed in virginal white lace panties and a bra paired with a pair of heels. It was a heady mix of sweetness and sin.

He stood and pulled off his shirt because he remembered how much she liked to touch his chest.

That's exactly where her hands went when he neared her.

While he would have loved to make love to her in nothing else but those heels, he slipped them from her feet and gently pushed on her shoulders so she'd lie down.

It didn't take him long to divest her of the rest of her clothes.

Back on his knees, he eased himself between her thighs and devoured her sweetness. In his mind, if he could relax her with an orgasm, she might not be as nervous.

When the first one peaked, crested and crashed, he stood up and removed his clothes. She sat up and stared at him. Her eyes took in his length and girth. He was right, he didn't see fear, he saw interest.

Her tiny hand slipped around him and he hissed at the feeling of finally being this close to making love to the only woman he'd ever loved.

"So soft and hard at the same time."

"First time to touch one?"

She nodded. "Yes, you get all my firsts."

"I'll take them." He shimmied them both up the bed. His body hovered over hers.

"I brought condoms."

He leaned toward the nightstand and took one out of the drawer. "I told you I'd take care of you. I bought these today." He rolled one on and positioned himself between her thighs. "Are you sure?" he asked because once he was inside her, he knew he'd want to live there forever.

She cupped his cheek and looked into his eyes with fierce love. "I've never been more certain of anything."

His heart was pounding so hard he was positive she'd hear it. He lined himself up. Her arousal created the lubrication they needed, and inch by inch he entered her.

She closed her eyes at the first pinch of pain.

"Don't do that. Look at me, Poppy."

She opened her eyes, and what he saw in the depths of hers filled his heart with so much emotion he wanted to cry. The love she had for him was plain to see.

"Let me love you. Let me see you."

She shifted her hips, pulling him deeper.

"Does it hurt?"

She shook her head. "No. It's tight and full."

He smiled. "Yes, it's tight all right." He pushed deeper until their hips met. "So damn tight." He pulled back and pushed forward slowly. "You okay?"

She lit up. "Yes, I'm perfect." Her hips moved on their own. She matched the rhythm he set. First slow, but as she adjusted, the pace and depth increased. She was like a velvet fist around him.

A shift in his position made her moan with pleasure. His arms shook as he tried to get her to the place he'd been for minutes—the edge. He prayed to the sex gods to give him stamina to last long enough to please her.

When her body tensed and her legs shook, when her nails clawed at his back and his name left her beautiful lips, he knew she'd made it, and it was time to follow her pleasure. His hips thrust forward until the only sound in the room was skin against skin followed by him calling her name.

Sweaty and sated, he rolled to his side and pulled her into his arms. "I love you. Thank you for making me your first."

She kissed him. "You'll be my last."

He pressed his forehead to hers and looked into her eyes. "You got that right. You're mine. All mine. Always mine." He got up to discard the condom, then returned from the bathroom with a damp, warm towel to clean her up.

Sliding in next to her, he held her close. This was the beginning of their forever.

And then her phone rang.

CHAPTER TWENTY

She jumped from the bed, racing naked into the living room in search of the phone. She found her purse on the chair.

Her fingers shook as she answered the call.

"Hello."

Mark was right behind her, hopping into his jeans as he approached.

"Oh, my God." Poppy didn't recognize her own voice. "I'm coming."

She hung up and ran back to the bedroom to grab her dress. She was a mess and struggled to get her arms into the sleeves. She fell to the floor in a heap.

Mark was there to catch her. He lifted her and sat her on the bed. "I've got you." He put on her bra and helped her into her underwear before he got her dress on and buttoned her up. He picked up her shoes and held her hand as he walked her to the door.

She was hyperventilating between sobs.

"Tell me what's going on."

"My mom is dying. She can't breathe. An ambulance is on the way."

"Okay." Before she knew it, she was in the cruiser. Mark had the lights flashing, and they were racing toward the ranch. "I'm here. We'll get through this together."

She buried her face in her hands and wept. "I should have never left her."

"She wanted you to go."

"I know, but that doesn't make it better. It doesn't make it right. While we were making love, she was dying. God, Mark I'll never forgive myself."

He held her hand but stayed silent. She knew deep inside she was wrong to blame herself and by association blame him. Her mother had told her to go. It was as if somehow, she'd known she'd be leaving tonight, and she wanted Poppy and Mark's relationship to be solidified.

When they approached, the ambulance was there and her mother was being wheeled out on a gurney. It broke her heart to see her like this. Doc was there telling the medics she had a DNR. Her father was there screaming for them to do anything so she would live. Violet was in their brother Basil's arms, crying.

Poppy did what she did best. She dried her tears and stood tall. She rushed over to her mother, who was hooked up to beeping, hissing machines and gave her a kiss good-bye. This was it, and she knew it. She leaned close to her mother's ear and whispered. "I love you. Thank you for being the best mom a girl could have." She'd always heard that people stayed until they knew their loved ones would be okay. Had her mother stayed to see her fall in love? To know that Mark would be here for her. If Poppy was okay, her mother knew she'd take care of everyone else. "It's okay if you have to go, Mom. We'll be fine. I promise." She had no idea if that was true but wouldn't let her mom know that.

Poppy moved aside as they raised the gurney into the ambulance. Her father climbed in the back.

"I'll get everyone to the hospital," said Mark.

They climbed into his cruiser and followed the flashing lights to Copper Creek. What normally took forty minutes took thirty, but when the back doors to the ambulance opened, none of it mattered.

Her mother lay still. The silence surrounding her said it all. Even her father didn't say a word. He climbed out of the back and walked away.

"Dad," Poppy called after him. "Dad, where are you going?"

He waved her off and disappeared into the night.

It was three in the morning when Mark drove them back to the ranch. Poppy had called her sisters and started to make the arrangements to get them home.

Basil and Violet went to their rooms, leaving Poppy alone with Mark.

"What do you need?" he asked.

She tugged at the roots of her hair and looked around the room. It still resembled a hospital. That would never do. Poppy didn't want to remember her mother the way she was this morning, hooked up to oxygen, lying in a hospital bed. She didn't want her sisters coming home from college to be greeted by despair. No. They would celebrate their mother's life. Remember the days when she rode the range with them. A happier time when they were an intact family. Then she thought about her father, who never had returned to the hospital. It was Poppy who'd started the process to bury her mother.

"Can you find my father and bring him home?"

Mark hugged her tight. "Yes, I can." He kissed the top of her head. "I've got you. You're not alone."

She melted into him. "Funny because I've never felt so alone in my life."

He thumbed her chin, so she would look at him. "You. Are. Not. Alone," he told her in no uncertain terms. After he placed a soft kiss to her lips, he said, "I love you. We're a team. We'll get through this together. You belong to me, and I take care of what's mine."

"I love you, but don't be upset if we can't be together for a bit. I've got so much to figure out." She felt him stiffen.

"I understand. Just remember, *we're* already figured out. Let's get your brother and sisters taken care of, and I'll find your father."

She walked him to the door and watched as he climbed into the cruiser and drove away.

She was wrong. That minute his taillights disappeared was the loneliest moment of her life.

The coffee brewed while she packed the medical supplies and put them on the porch. As soon as a decent hour to call hit, she called the clinic and asked if they could pick up the equipment. It was hard enough knowing her mother was gone but having to look at the reminders was pure torture.

Her father hadn't returned but thankfully he'd left the keys to his truck.

"Why me?" asked Basil, when she asked him to pick up his sisters from the airport.

She stomped her foot and fisted her hips. She was tired. Tired of being responsible for everything. Tired of having to bear the bulk of the burden. She knew Basil and Violet had sacrificed too, but as the oldest, she had more years under her belt and they owed her.

"Because I can't do it all. Lily and Daisy can't walk from Denver. Rose is on her way. Stop complaining."

"Don't we get time to grieve?" he asked.

"Yes, you can grieve the rest of your life, but right now you're going to pitch in because it's what Mom would want. I promised her we'd be okay, and we will if we help each other, and right now what I need is for you to get to the airport."

Basil held out his hand for the keys and she opened the coffee jar where she put her cashed paychecks. Mom wouldn't need meds anymore, but the truck would need gas. She gave him a hundred dollars and reminded him to feed them on their way home.

As he walked out, the townsfolk started showing up.

Sage and Marina arrived with cleaning supplies. "Doc said you were straightening up the place; we thought we'd help."

Next to arrive was Louise Williams. It was the first time Poppy could remember seeing her when Louise wasn't pregnant. Instead of a baby in her arms, she had a stack of casserole dishes.

"I froze a few just in case of emergencies." She walked into the kitchen like she'd been there a thousand times and yet Poppy didn't think she'd ever been to the ranch at all.

Abby arrived with candles and lotions and aromatherapy oils. "Lavender is calming," she said. She went to work next to Marina and Sage.

Cannon, Bowie, and Luke came with a truck full of lumber and a jar filled with donations. "Thought we'd finish up the list. Anything you need right away?" Luke asked.

A lump too big to swallow nearly choked her. Here were the people not related to her pitching in to do the dirty work, and her own father was missing in action. She knew he was suffering but he didn't need to do it alone. Looking around at how the people of Aspen Cove circled the wagons, she realized she didn't have to do it alone either.

Violet walked downstairs, carrying Mom's favorite dress. It was a pink floral that she always wore in the summer.

"I think she'd like this." Poor Violet's voice cracked. As the youngest, she'd suffer the most. Poppy needed to remind herself that her sister was only eighteen. Right then, she knew how lucky she'd been to have her mother for ten years longer.

"She'd love that. You did a great job. You want to get her jewelry together?"

Violet nodded. "What should I get?"

"How about a necklace, those flower earrings she loved, and her wedding band."

With something to do, Violet raced back upstairs only to come back moments later to say she couldn't find her mother's wedding ring.

Poppy hugged her sister. "Don't worry, I'm sure Dad knows where it is."

The last to arrive at the house was Katie, who arrived with boxes of muffins and cookies. She put them on the counter and handed Poppy her car keys. "You'll need extra wheels when everyone is here."

"I can't take your car."

"Sure, you can. We've got two. Use it for as long as you need it."

Two hours later Poppy was alone again. Only this time her heart didn't feel so hollow. She flopped onto the couch and looked around. All the medical equipment was gone. The house was spotless. It smelled like tamale casserole because one was warming in the oven.

Violet joined her on the sofa. She curled up next to

Poppy and cried. And just like her mother would have done, Poppy held her close and told her it would be okay. Deep inside she now believed that to be true. In a single day, she'd experienced the highest of highs when Mark truly claimed her and the lowest of lows when her mother died. Two opposing emotions connected by the thread of love.

She reached for her phone and texted him.

I miss you.

He texted back.

I miss you too. Still searching for your dad.

CHAPTER TWENTY-ONE

Finding Lloyd Dawson was like finding a needle in a haystack. It was an impossible task but one he'd accomplish for Poppy. It pissed Mark off that during one of the most vulnerable moments for the Dawsons, their father was MIA.

Mark shouldn't be combing the streets and the trails for him. He should be supporting the woman he loved. While he was searching, Poppy was doing what Poppy did, she took care of everyone, but there was no one taking care of her. The asshole could rot in hell as far as Mark was concerned, but Poppy wanted him found and he'd do whatever she wanted.

After letting Aiden know what he was up to, Mark called in favors at all the surrounding towns, starting with the new police chief of Copper Creek since that was where Lloyd had walked away from his family.

Every bar, and hotel were checked out. The parks came up empty too. If Lloyd had taken to the trails, there was no way they'd find him. Without food or water, his chances for survival were slim. Then it hit him. Lloyd would have gone to the place he felt comfortable. A place that felt like home and provided a cloak of safety.

He packed his car with some provisions and drove to the backroad that led onto the Dawsons' property. Something told Mark he was at one of the cabins. It should have been the first place they looked, but with him disappearing forty miles away it didn't seem likely.

There were five safety shelters on the range. The first two he visited hadn't seen a human in years, but they had seen a few raccoons and a rodent or two. The third cabin was where his father had spent many a drunken night. It was nothing more than a pile of lumber, and Mark wondered if Lloyd had torn it down after their falling-out.

He drove his cruiser over the rough terrain along the outskirts of the ranch. The sky was blue with not a cloud in sight. Up ahead a few antelope grazed in the open field, taking their fill before the Dawsons' herd was moved to this part of the land.

Lloyd was always conscientious about moving his cattle regularly so as not to strip the land bare. Mark remembered a time when cattle could be seen from any place on the range. Not so much anymore or for the past several decades.

Lloyd had sold off most of his herd and kept it small. It was a wonder how they'd survived.

Off in the distance, he saw the cabin he called the smoking cabin. Things were looking good as he approached, since the door was ajar.

Mark parked the cruiser. He debated leaving his weapon in the car for safety reasons, but whose safety was he concerned about? If Lloyd was armed and drunk, then he'd need his weapon. Then again, he knew no matter what, he'd never pull a weapon on Poppy's father.

He unstrapped his belt and tucked it under the seat out of sight and out of the way.

A shadow fell across the open door and Lloyd leaned against the doorframe.

Mark exited the cruiser and walked forward.

Lloyd took a menacing step toward him. The piece of hay he'd been chewing fell to the ground. "You don't belong here, son. This ain't your land."

Mark had a lot of ways to play this. He could take on the role of deputy sheriff and tell Lloyd he was doing his job. He could say he was a concerned friend of the family. The truth was he wouldn't have given a rat's ass where Lloyd had disappeared to if it hadn't been for Poppy. "I was invited onto your land. Your children are looking for you."

"You tell them I'm fine."

Lloyd looked anything but fine. It had only been just over a day since Carol died, and yet Lloyd looked like he'd aged ten years. His clothes were dirty and wrinkled. A smattering of gray whiskers shadowed his face. His eyes had lost the light they'd had in them. Even if the only light Mark saw was a flame of fury, it was gone.

Mark turned around and walked back to the cruiser. He had no intention of leaving. It was his goal to bring Lloyd back to the house, but if that didn't work out, he was going to leave the man provisions.

He opened the back of the cruiser and picked up a box he'd put together. Inside was a can of Lloyd's favorite chew, a six-pack of cold beer, several cans of chili, a box of crackers and some candy bars. "I brought you some supplies."

Lloyd's eyes opened wide before they narrowed. "A box of groceries will never make up for what your father stole from me."

Mark shook his head. Poor Lloyd had been stuck on replay for the past two decades and on some level so had he. He'd let the bitterness of a grown man mold his life.

He walked the box to the small cabin and set it on the step. Fishing inside, he found the can of chew and handed it to Lloyd. He pulled off two cans of beer, popped the tops and handed one to the man who'd made his life worse than his father could have.

"First off, I could never pay you back for what my father stole from you." He took a seat and looked up at the man he'd once wished was his father.

Lloyd glanced at the beer in his hand. "Looks like you're more like him than not." He took a look at the watch on his wrist. "Your pop didn't believe waiting until noon either." He nodded at Mark's uniform. "He drank on the job too."

Mark chuckled. It was ten minutes to noon and drinking on the job was not a habit he had. In fact, he couldn't recall a time when he ever had a drink in uniform, but today was different.

"I'm not actually on duty. I went in for a few hours and then took the rest of the day off to find you."

"What if I don't want to be found." He brought the can of beer to his lips and drank.

"Too late. What's done is done." Mark took a sip and put the can on the step beside him. "Why don't you have a seat. I won't take up too much of your time."

Lloyd opened the can of chew and shoved a pinch into his mouth. "Thank you for this." He held up the can before he shoved it into his back pocket and took a seat. "Times a ticking so say what you gotta say and be gone."

Sitting this close, Mark could see that Lloyd had shed a river of tears. His eyes were red-rimmed and swollen.

Mark kicked out his feet and looked off into the range. "When I was a kid, I used to pretend you were my father. You were such a good man. Always loving. Always patient. Always kind." He picked up his beer and took a long drink. "I'm sorry my father stole that from you. I'm sorrier that he stole that from your kids." The bubbles rose up to a burp he couldn't suppress. "Excuse me," he said. "By the way, all your children are at home waiting for you. I'm here because Poppy asked me to find you."

"You always do what she says?"

While he hadn't in the past, he knew he'd always do what she wanted in the future. Since he started paying close attention to what Poppy wanted, his life had been full. Full of shitty situations like Lloyd but full of love.

"Not in the past but I will in the future. Didn't you listen to Carol?"

The mention of her name made them both pause. As if on cue they lowered their heads.

"She was a good woman." Lloyd's voice cracked.

"Yes, she was. She raised five beautiful girls and a son."

Lloyd spit it the dusty ground to his side. "You don't get to talk about my family."

Mark was so damn tired of Lloyd's rules. "Fine, then I'll talk about mine." He shifted so he could look Lloyd in the eye. "I was eight when my father robbed you blind and left. Eight years old when he abandoned my mother and me, but you know what? That wasn't what hurt the most." He kicked at the dirt beneath his feet. He'd never talked like this to anyone. "It was when you abandoned me that I was crushed."

"Me?"

Mark nodded his head. "Yes, I didn't expect much from

my father. He was a drunk. A mean drunk. He was a lousy husband, and a worse father but you... I expected a whole hell of a lot more from you. When you turned your back on us, I was broken. Eight years old and the only man I ever respected let me down. That man wasn't Mick Bancroft, it was you."

Lloyd's eyes never left him. "Your father—"

Mark held up his hand. "He was an asshole. He was a drunk. He was a womanizer. None of those things were secrets. Everyone knew including you and yet...you hired him anyway. Why is that my fault? You have a history of making poor decisions."

Lloyd set his beer down and fisted his palms.

Mark was certain he'd throw a punch, but he'd gladly take it if it helped.

"You don't have a right to come onto my land and disrespect me."

Maybe egging the man on wasn't the wisest of choices but something drastic had to happen. He thought losing Carol might make Lloyd see how much time he'd wasted being angry and bitter. He was wrong.

"Let me tell you about myself." He laid his hands flat on his thighs as a sign of peace. "I was raised by a single mother who demanded I always tell the truth. Once my father was gone, she set out to make sure I understood how a real man should behave. She once told me that when I fell in love, she wanted me to be the prince my girl dreamed about. Poppy is my girl. I've loved her longer than I can remember. I was in love with her before I could saddle my own horse, but after my father left, the message that was planted in my head by you was that I was worth less than the dung on your boots."

"You'll never be good enough for Poppy." Lloyd finished

off his beer and crushed the can, then tossed it aside before he grabbed another.

"You're right. I'll never be good enough for her because she's that amazing. Despite you and your egotistical and stubborn ways, she turned out to be a remarkable woman. I'd say that's because of Carol."

"Do you have a point?"

Mark nodded his head. "Yes, I do. While I'll never be good enough, I'll never stop trying, which makes me different from you. It makes me better than you because you stopped trying the day my father left. Have you taken a look in the mirror lately?"

Lloyd jumped to his feet. "Don't you dare."

"What? Don't be honest?" Mark stood so Lloyd wouldn't have to reach too far if he wanted to throw the punch. "You turned into the man you hated. You turned into my father. You abandoned your ranch. You abandoned your family. You're doing it again because Carol died. Your kids need you. They need you to be the man of the family. Isn't it high time Poppy stopped wearing the pants?"

Mark closed his eyes and waited for the impact of Lloyd's fist but nothing came, so he continued. "I learned how to be a man from watching you." He let out a deep sigh. "Please don't turn out to be less of a man than I think you are."

He stepped off the porch and walked toward his cruiser. Before he climbed inside, he stared back at Lloyd. "I love your daughter. I will marry her. I'll take care of her and love her until the day I die. You can hate me, but don't make her choose between you and me. Neither one of us can handle that kind of loss."

Lloyd didn't say a thing. He merely let his head drop until his chin almost touched his chest.

"I'll tell them you're safe. Don't keep them waiting. They may be adults, but they'll never stop needing their father. When will the Lloyd Dawson I knew and loved return?"

As soon as the tiny structure was a dot in his rearview mirror, he called Poppy.

CHAPTER TWENTY-TWO

Although Mark called yesterday to tell Poppy her father was at his cabin, it wasn't until this afternoon that he'd shown up looking worn and tired.

"I'm going to take a shower, and then we'll have a family meeting."

Poppy's eyes nearly bugged out. The last time she could recall them having a family meeting was when her mother received the ALS diagnosis. She hoped this meeting wouldn't have such dire consequences.

She picked up her phone and called Mark. He'd wanted to come by yesterday evening but she'd told him she was exhausted. That was the truth but not the whole of it. She was simply overwhelmed with everything and didn't know how to handle how their last night ended. While he drove her to her house after they'd made love, she'd told him she regretted it because while he was giving her so much pleasure her mother was dying.

The weight of that guilt sat heavy on her heart. As did the guilt of telling her mother that it was okay to go. The doctors assured her that her mother didn't give up—her body did. She'd lasted far longer than most people with her condition, but that information didn't help. Carol Dawson was still gone, and Poppy and Mark's first time making love would always be tainted with that memory.

Fifteen minutes later, her father came downstairs. He looked around the living room, which was spotless.

All six of his children were present. They were lined up around the living room in order of birth, with Poppy taking up the end of the couch. Violet, the youngest, sat on the floor in front of her.

"You've been busy."

He plopped into the recliner that was always his. No one sat in it but her father. No one dared.

Lloyd palmed his freshly shaved face. His eyes were tired, but there was something inside them Poppy hadn't seen in a long time—hope.

"I thought maybe we could order a pizza and have a family dinner?"

All six mouths surrounding him dropped open. Poppy was the only one to respond. "We have enough casseroles and food to last for months. Why don't I put one in the oven?"

Her father nodded.

An hour later they sat at the big kitchen table. Carol's seat was empty except for a picture Rose had placed there. It was the last family photo they had taken together. Poor little Violet hadn't even been born.

Lloyd saw she was missing and pulled a picture of Carol and Violet from his wallet and leaned it against the frame so everyone was accounted for.

"Your mom would have loved this." His voice fractured. He cleared his throat several times. "She did love family meals. I was thinking we could go around the table and share our favorite Mom stories." Lloyd wiped a stray tear from his eyes.

Poppy couldn't remember ever seeing her father cry. The act made him more human. While she'd been so frustrated at him over the past few weeks—hell, the past few years—she realized now that her father had been hiding from his feelings.

Everyone told a heartwarming story about family and love, particularly about the undying love their mother had for anything and everyone.

They ate tamale pie and laughed and cried. At the end, her father apologized.

"I'm sorry for everything I did and everything I didn't do, but the one thing I'll never be sorry for is all of you. When I look at you, I see your mother." He took a deep breath. "I have a lot of regrets. I wish I'd have been a better man. A stronger man." He sipped his water and took a moment to look at each one of them. He ended on Poppy. "I asked a lot from my kids and returned very little." He pushed his empty plate forward. "I met with a young man yesterday."

They all knew who he was talking about. Mark was the only person who knew where their father had disappeared to. He'd told Poppy to give her father some time to come to terms with everything. When he did, Mark was certain Lloyd would come home.

"This person knows what it's like to be disappointed in people. The ones closest to him had left him to fend for himself. He pointed out that while I might have been present physically in your lives, I was absent emotionally. He also pointed out that the sins of the father should never be passed on to the child."

Her father swallowed hard like he was choking on

something. "Things have to change here. You have lives to live. You can't live mine." His eyes fell on Rose, Lily, and Daisy. "You three owe your sisters and a brother a debt of gratitude." He laid his hand on the table. "I got a call today from Doc. He said I was supposed to look under the mattress on your mother's side of the bed." He reached behind him and pulled out a stapled packet of papers. "While I wasn't looking, your mother invested in life insurance." He slipped a piece of stationery from the pages and once again cleared his throat.

My Dearest Lloyd,

That sounds almost insincere coming from me. How about we start again.

My burning hunk of love,

Get your ass out of your head. Yes, I did mean that. You've turned into a walking asshole, but you're still lovable and redeemable.

If you're reading this, it's because I was right. All those days in the saddle didn't cause the tingling, numbness, and muscle weakness. I was always a sneaky one. I managed to get you even when you had eyes for Penny Larson. I knew then as I do now that we were meant to be together. Just look at our children and you can see the truth.

I bought this policy hoping that someday I could help right a wrong. I could turn what turned out to be twenty years of hell into a lifetime of heaven. Turn the other cheek and start over. Life is too damn short. Take the money and do the right thing.

I love you. Always have...always will.

Love,

Carol (the flame that kept you burning)

When her father folded the paper, there wasn't a dry eye in the place.

Basil spoke first. "What's the right thing?"

All eyes watched the head of the table.

"Your mother managed to pay for an insurance policy all these years. It's a half million dollars."

There were collective gasps from around the table.

"You have a half million dollars?" Violet asked.

Despite the somber situation, Lloyd smiled. "No, we have a half million dollars."

Again, Basil asked, "What's the right thing to do?"

"We're a family and that decision will be made as a family. First things are first, we need to bury your mother and the love of my life. She deserves lots of flowers. I never gave her enough of them while she was alive."

Violet raised her hand like she was in school. "Yes, you did, you gave her an entire bouquet with a little spice added in. Every day of her life she had Poppies, Roses, Lilies, Daisies, and Violets with a sprig of fabulous Basil. We were a living, breathing bouquet."

Lloyd broke down into tears.

TWO DAYS later they buried their mother. The funeral was held in Copper Creek, but the burial was in Aspen Cove. It was a warm, sunny day. The sky was blue. Birds chirped overhead while Carol Dawson was lowered into the ground. Their father had ordered dozens of flowers. All the girls' namesakes were accounted for as was a wreath made exclusively from basil.

Doc officiated at the gravesite, like he normally did. He was the go-to guy for everything from medical care to property sales. He'd married most of the people in town including Poppy's parents. He'd delivered ninety percent of the children in town too. It seemed fitting that if he brought people into the world, he should be the one to send them out as well.

"I met with Carol many times during her illness. She had specific requests. One of them was for you to all get your asses to the Brewhouse and raise a pint in her honor. Those were her exact words. I'll meet you there." He started to walk away but pointed at the Dawson children. "I have a gift from your mother. Don't dawdle." He looked at Lloyd. "You too."

After the last handful of dirt was thrown and the flowers were neatly placed across the gravesite, they all made their way to the Brewhouse.

Sage and Katie had already poured several pitchers of beer when the Dawsons arrived. Aspen Cove took care of their own, which meant there was enough food to feed an army and enough alcohol to numb a nation.

Doc climbed onto the karaoke stage and tapped the microphone. "I've got one job to do." He opened a yellow sheet of paper and took out his glasses.

Poppy stood to the side until she felt a warm hand grasp hers. Next to her stood Mark. He leaned in and whispered. "I love you. I've given you all the space I can. Don't ask me to give you more. I want to be here for you."

Worried that old habits would die hard, she looked to her right where her father stood. She half expected to see a frown, but there wasn't one. All Lloyd Dawson did was nod and turn his attention back to Doc.

Doc adjusted his glasses. Once perched on his nose, he began. "These are not my words," he said, and then read the letter.

Many of you will question my family. You will wonder

why they didn't try everything. Why I didn't have home health care. Why I wasn't in a long-term care facility.

That decision wasn't theirs to make. It was mine.

Many will look at Lloyd with suspicion. They'll think he didn't love me enough to sacrifice. The opposite is true. He was willing to give it all up to find a cure.

I want to be surrounded by the land I love, and the people who make it perfect. My children are the greatest gift I've ever received. It never mattered how much money we do and don't have, I'm the richest woman because of them.

My husband is a proud man. He silently suffers and hides behind a mask of indifference. It's just a mask. Don't let him fool you.

Raise your pints and toast to love. It's the most valuable asset on earth.

I love you all, but dammit. Get off your asses and live like there's no tomorrow. You never know. There might not be.

With love,

Carol

Everyone raised their glasses and toasted to love.

Doc stepped down from the stage and walked to Poppy and her siblings. Out of a bigger envelope, he pulled eight smaller ones.

One was given to each Dawson child, one was given to Lloyd. The final envelope was slid into Mark's hand.

No one seemed to be in a hurry to read what was written. It was because the letters would be like a final conversation with Carol. One that should be had in private.

CHAPTER TWENTY-THREE

Mark drove Poppy home after the funeral and reception. His poor girl looked exhausted. He wanted to stay and hold her, hug her, kiss her, but her poor lids drooped heavier with each passing moment.

It seemed as if Lloyd and he had reached a gentleman's agreement, or maybe Lloyd was also too tired to fight because when Mark asked for permission to take Poppy upstairs and get her settled, Lloyd didn't argue.

Poppy made it to the first step when she turned around. "Dad, in the commotion, I forgot to tell you that Mom's wedding ring is missing."

Lloyd's eyes went straight to Mark. He was certain the next thing out of his mouth would be an accusation. That somehow during the last conversation he'd had with Carol that he'd stolen it because in Lloyd's eyes he was just like his father. That didn't happen. Lloyd sat in his recliner and said, "It will show up. Don't you worry."

Mark took Poppy's hand in his and led her to her room. He'd only been there once as a boy. It was a day when Poppy was sick and Carol asked Mark's mother to bring him over. He went upstairs and cheered her up. Lloyd wasn't happy that day, but Carol got her way and he got to spend a few hours with the girl of his dreams.

That was the day she beat him several times in the game of Sorry, but he wasn't sorry. He knew right then she was the one. How could he not love someone who sat there in pigtails and freckles and told him that someday he was going to marry her?

His mom always told him that women were always right and men should always be sorry. He thought it was bullshit, but now he wondered if his mother was right.

Poppy fell to her bed as soon as she walked into her room. She patted the space beside her. "I need to tell you something." She scooted over to make room for him.

He looked at the door, half expecting Lloyd to be standing there with his shotgun. When he wasn't, Mark climbed onto the bed with her. She curled into a ball next to him.

"I'm so tired. I think I need to sleep for a week."

He brushed back the hair that had fallen over her beautiful face. "I love you. I'm here for you. If you need to sleep a week, you should. You deserve to take a break."

She rolled her neck. After a few pops, she looked up at him with her big green eyes. "I'm sorry I pushed you away."

"It's okay. I know you were busy."

She shook her head. "No, that's not it. I felt guilty."

He leaned forward and touched her forehead with his. "About the night we made love?"

She nodded, making his head move with hers. "Yes, but not because we made love. That was my initial response but in truth, it was because it was so amazing and I never told you how good it was for me. I never told you how much I appreciated your patience. Your tender loving care. While I did feel guilty about being away from my mother, I realize now that's what she wanted. She wanted me to find love before she died." Poppy swiped a tear from her eye. "I always knew I loved you but that night... That was everything. Thank you."

Mark had a hard time not crying. He'd also felt guilty about taking her away from her mother but he'd promised Carol. She was adamant that he take Poppy out. Her exact words were, "Take her home and show her what love feels like. Give her a glimpse of her forever." While Carol could hardly speak, she'd made sure those words were clear. He'd made the promise. A promise he'd keep again if time rewound itself.

"As soon as things settle down, we'll have a do-over. A night of love and laughter."

"And sex. Lots of sex."

Mark laughed. "Yes, lots of sex. Now let's get you tucked into bed."

She slipped on a nightgown that, despite it coming to her neck and down to her ankles, made him hard.

He pulled the covers to her chin. The only things stopping him from crawling between the sheets were Lloyd and the fact that she truly looked ready to drop.

"I opened my mom's letter when I snuck off to the bathroom in the Brewhouse," she whispered.

He didn't want to admit that he'd done the same. "Yeah? Was it good?"

She smiled. "Yes, she told me it was okay to chase my dreams and to fall in love."

"I'm so glad, Poppy. Your mother was a blessing to us all."

"Did you read yours?"

He could have lied but he didn't. "Yes, I snuck off to the bathroom at the Brewhouse too."

She laughed. "We are two pods from the same pea."

He couldn't stop himself from doubling over. "You mean two peas from the same pod."

"Mark Bancroft." She got her older sibling voice on, or it was her unhappy girlfriend. "You're not supposed to point out my errors. I'm tired."

He cupped her face and touched her lips gently with his. "You're right. You'll always be right, Poppy."

She turned into his hand and kissed his palm. "Glad we agree. Now, are you going to tell me what my mother said?"

"She told me to love you. She told me to give you the life you deserve. A life of pictures, picnics, and babies. I'll pick you up tomorrow. Bring your camera."

She perked up. "Will we go to the overlook again?" She squirmed in bed.

There might have been exhaustion in her eyes, sorrow in her heart, but Poppy was full of unbridled passion.

"I'll take you wherever you want to go." He leaned down and kissed her. It wasn't a simple peck on the lips. It was a promise of more.

When Mark walked downstairs, he looked at Lloyd. "You leaving?"

"Yes, sir." He took his keys from the pocket of his dark suit trousers. "Thank you for letting me say goodnight."

He nodded.

Just as Mark reached for the door handle, Lloyd spoke again.

"I'd like to stop by your house in the morning and speak man to man."

Mark's heart thumped wildly. "I'll make the coffee. What time will you be by?"

"Sunrise. No use wasting the daylight."

Mark chuckled. "Spoken like a true rancher." He looked at the shotgun leaning against the wall. "Leave your gun at home."

"Afraid I'm as good a shot as everyone says?"

"Yes." Mark walked out and closed the door before Lloyd could say anything else, but the man's laughter followed him all the way to his car.

AT FIVE IN THE MORNING, Mark was sitting on his porch with two cups of steaming coffee when Lloyd Dawson pulled up.

His made his way to the front and took a seat.

"You know why I'm here?"

Mark couldn't say for sure. "Hoping it's not to beat my ass for something."

Lloyd reached out and patted him on the back. "Nope. Real men admit when they're wrong. Smart men do it before their wives die."

He took a yellow piece of paper from his pocket. In the center, a piece was missing as if something had been attached and stripped away.

He laid the paper on his thigh and pressed the wrinkles out the best he could with his palms. "I thought about this all afternoon and all night." He looked down at the paper that had few words.

Lloyd,

I love you more than you could know. Inside is my wedding ring. You know what to do with it.

No, you won't give it to your next wife. Someday you

should have a new wife. Someone who will love and care for you and our children like I did. You deserve that.

As for the ring. Do the right thing.

I'll love you forever,

Carol

"Carol used that phrase a lot. 'Do the right thing,' she'd say if we were ever tossed and torn. Funny thing is, the right thing was always what she wanted. She didn't act selfishly or without care for what others wanted or needed. She acted with compassion and love." Lloyd reached into his shirt pocket and pulled out a ring. It was a simple solitaire with a gold band. "I gave this to Carol the day we graduated high school. I think I always knew I'd marry her. She told me I would when we were in seventh grade."

Mark chuckled. "Poppy was eight when she told me."

Lloyd shook his head. "The Dawson women are smart and...they're always right."

"I'm learning that." Mark sipped his coffee and handed Lloyd the other cup.

"You better learn fast. It's a painful lesson if you don't." He looked down at the ring that looked tiny in his big hands. "She said to do the right thing." He reached out and put the ring in Mark's hand. "This belongs on Poppy's finger. It carries a legacy of love. Carol always loved you. She told me once that you two would get married. That day I wanted to shoot myself but...she was right. I was wrong. I'm sorry Mark." He looked around the front yard. "You've got yourself a nice setup here. You've worked hard to establish yourself as a good man. I ignored everything. I chose to see you differently because it allowed me to wallow in my stupidity and misery longer. I hope you'll accept my apology, and if you're serious about marrying my daughter, I hope you'll accept her mother's ring."

The morning light hit the diamond just right to send prisms of light across the deck. Every color of the rainbow was represented. Somehow it felt like Carol had just smiled. "I will marry your daughter. I would have done it without your approval but now that you're here, I'd like to ask your permission to marry Poppy."

Mark's insides twisted and turned. His hand held an apology but it was the yes from Lloyd's lips that would make it all real. The ring was from Carol, the rest would have to come from Lloyd.

"Show me your place. I want to see what my daughter's getting out of the deal before I say yes."

They stood and Mark opened the door to his home. A home he'd never imagined Lloyd Dawson would step a foot in.

CHAPTER TWENTY-FOUR

Poppy paced the porch, waiting for Mark. She rushed around the ranch to get her chores done. Her sisters had climbed into Katie's Jeep and taken off toward Silver Springs, while her father had disappeared. It was Basil who told her he'd gone to visit Mark.

She'd texted him at least a half dozen times to make sure he was okay. While her father had been kind and tolerant yesterday, she wasn't sure if it was lasting.

Down the gravel road, a cloud of dust kicked up. First to come into her line of sight was her father's truck followed by Mark's cruiser.

"Good afternoon, Poppy," her dad said as he passed her on his way into the house.

Mark rushed forward and picked her up, swinging her in a circle for a hug. "You ready?"

Poppy felt like she was living in an alternate reality.

"Did you spend the morning with my father?"

He nodded. "We had coffee and a chat. He didn't stay long because he had to pay the insurance company a visit."

"You had a chat?" She ran her hands up his back.

"Checking for holes?" He walked her down the stairs and helped her into the passenger seat. "I'm in one piece. No blood was shed." He rounded the car and climbed in. "You've got options. We can go to the overlook and have a picnic lunch but no sex." He watched her.

"No sex?"

He put the car in gear and drove off. "I talked to Trig today. He said the trail is busy during the day, and if we wanted privacy, we should go somewhere else."

Her mouth dropped open. "He knows we're having sex?" Her cheeks flushed with heat.

"No, he just figured with the funeral and all, maybe you wanted someplace quiet and peaceful."

"So where do you want to take me?"

He reached over to hold her hand. "Home, I want to take you home."

She smiled broadly. "We're going to have sex, right?"

"What is it with you and sex."

She stuck her lower lip out in a pout. "It's been a cruddy few weeks. Actually, a few years, and the best times I've had were with you. The happiest I've been has been when I'm with you, wrapped in your arms."

"Well, then. Let's get you home and make you happy."

It didn't escape her notice that he said home and continued to drive into town.

When they arrived at his place, he took her straight to bed, where he made her happy all afternoon and into the evening.

Later that night he drove her to the ranch with a promise to stop by on his next day off, which wasn't for three days.

At the prospect of not seeing Mark for three days, she

felt like she couldn't breathe, but she had her whole family at the ranch and she needed to spend time with them too.

They were sitting at the table playing board games, and by the gleam in her dad's eyes, he was winning. When their game was finished, he called another family meeting. One where they took a vote on how to spend the insurance money.

Since her sisters were on scholarships, they had no debts to clear. What they all desperately needed were cars. After Lloyd agreed to buy them all vehicles, the kids voted for what would happen to the rest of the money. This was one time where being a child of Lloyd Dawson worked in their favor. He was outvoted six to one.

Their mother loved the ranch. It had been in her family for decades. Their plan was to make sure the ranch would expand and grow. Aspen Cove was a thriving town, and with growth came opportunity for all who lived nearby.

Lloyd agreed to hire external help so his children could chase their dreams. Lily, Daisy, and Rose would return to college. Violet would help out at the ranch until the end of summer, when she'd enter an overseas volunteer program. She didn't care if she taught English to Tibetan monks or helped build wells for poverty-stricken villagers in South America. All she wanted to do was travel.

Basil wanted to chase his dream too. Or rather, chase girls. He was happy at the ranch and had never considered a life outside of riding horses, taking cooking lessons from Dalton, and raising cattle. As for Poppy? She'd stay put too. Nothing made her happier than her moments with Mark.

CHAPTER TWENTY-FIVE

Weeks had passed and life was settling into a new normal.

Mark was dirty from head to toe after a long day of helping Lloyd on the ranch. He'd started filling in one day a week until the new foreman, Wyatt Morrison, arrived from Montana. He was coming from the Starling Ranch.

A shadow crossed the barn door. Poppy leaned against the frame and smiled. She raised her camera and snapped a few pictures. The damn woman was like the paparazzi with that camera. Most women wore jewelry, Poppy wore a Nikon.

He stood and stared at her. With the bright light behind her, it was as if she was wrapped in the sun. She was so damn sexy in blue jeans and boots. On their next happy day, he was determined to have her naked but wearing those boots.

"You stalking me?" He tossed the last bale of hay and wiped his hands on his jeans.

"I've been stalking you since I could walk. Are you only noticing now?" She pushed off the wood frame and made her way to him. It didn't take long for her lips to crash into his and for his arms to circle her waist.

They were deep into a passionate kiss when he heard a throat clear.

Poppy hopped back.

Mark laughed.

She was still skittish when it came to showing affection in front of her father. It was as if she expected him to grab his gun any second and chase Mark from the property. That wasn't going to happen.

When Lloyd visited him that day at his house, Mark had reminded him that he had every intention of marrying Poppy. Lloyd hadn't argued. Maybe there was some leeway given because they were in Mark's house. Or it was simply because Lloyd realized he would lose this battle.

One thing was certain though, Lloyd was on board. His only request had been that Mark use Carol's ring to propose, and that he wait a few weeks so Poppy could get past the newness of losing her mother.

Lloyd didn't want her engagement to forever be connected to Carol's death.

"I thought you were working?" Lloyd said in a tone of mock irritation. After spending more time with him, Mark could tell when he was genuinely unhappy or just pulling someone's leg.

"I was," Mark says. "I was working on making your daughter happy."

Lloyd shook his head. "Impossible task. She's like her mother. You'll be working at the happiness quotient for the rest of your life."

Mark pulled Poppy to his front, wrapped his arms around her waist, then set his chin on her shoulder. "That's a good problem to have."

"You know that thing we talked about?" Lloyd lifted his brows.

"Yes, sir."

"It's about time, don't you think?"

Mark couldn't contain his smile. "Yes, sir."

Poppy twisted in his arms. "You're talking code like you're best buddies?"

Lloyd walked over and yanked on Poppy's ponytail. "You won't let me kill him. What other choice do I have?" Lloyd laughed and threw his arm around Mark's shoulder. "Besides, he's a hard worker, and I'd expect nothing less from one of my sons." Lloyd started for the door.

Mark attempted to kiss the shocked look off Poppy's face. "Sorry for the dirt, sweetheart."

"Get a room," Lloyd said as he walked out the door.

"Good idea." He pulled away and looked at his beautiful woman. "How about I go home, take a shower, and you meet me there in an hour."

"How about I go home with you and we shower together. Saves time and water."

It wasn't part of his plan, but the idea had merit. He and Poppy were experiencing all kinds of firsts together. Up until now, they'd never made love in the shower. He was already hard thinking about it.

"Meet me at the cruiser in five minutes."

She let out a squeal and rushed from the barn.

While he waited for her, he called Trig and reserved another four-wheeler. It seemed fitting that he'd ask her to marry him where they'd had their first date.

Ten minutes later Poppy raced out of the house with a bag.

"You're late," he told her.

"I was trying to find that black and red lingerie you

like." She took the thin strip of fabric from her bag and held it up.

"You're forgiven." He put the car in gear and rushed home.

They left a trail of clothes from the front door to the bathroom. Mark never tired of seeing Poppy naked. She had flawless skin. So pale that even his kisses left a trail of red wherever his lips touched. He turned on the water and while he waited for it to warm, he heated up Poppy. It didn't take much to get her going. She was a passionate and willing partner. When he dropped to his knees in front of her, she moaned before his tongue even touched her.

"You're going to spoil me."

He pulled back and licked his lips. She always tasted sweet like honey. "Going to? You're already spoiled, but I plan to up my game."

She leaned against the counter and threaded her fingers through his hair. His favorite thing about arousing Poppy was the little sounds she made. How her knees shook and weakened, and how at the pinnacle of her pleasure she always called his name.

He ate up her pleasure and carried her into the shower. With both of them under the stream, they let the water sluice over their bodies. Though she was sated, she was always ready for more. Was it because she had so much time to make up for?

"Have I told you I love you today?"

She leaned against his chest and wrapped her arms around his waist. His obvious arousal, trapped between their bodies, throbbed for relief.

"About a hundred times, but I'll be happy to hear it a hundred more. There aren't enough lifetimes to get tired of those words."

She moved her hand between their bodies. Her tiny fingers gripped his steely length and stroked a deep groan from his throat.

"You're killing me."

She shook her head. "No, I'm loving you."

He lifted her up so she could wrap her legs around his waist. He lined himself up and found her eyes. Pools of emerald green looked at him with lust and love. The position was perfect to slide right in.

"Mmm," she moaned.

Identical sounds flowed from him. Slow, soft strokes brought them both to the edge. "Have I thanked you for going on the pill?" He pressed her back against the tiles and picked up his pace and pressure.

"You can show me how thankful you are."

Poppy gripped his shoulders, her body tightened and stilled as her nails dug into his skin, intensifying his pleasure. Driven by lust and need, he thrust into her again and again. A rush of heat tightened in his core. He was on the edge, hoping and praying she'd catch up to him. When her legs pulled him deeper and her moans got louder, he thanked the heavens.

"I love you, Poppy." When he felt her pulse around his length, he thrust deep inside. The grip she had on him pushed him over the top.

Once every quake and quiver left them, she slowly slid from his body.

He suds'd her up. He washed her hair and told her all the ways he'd love her forever. While he didn't expect her to say no, he wanted to make sure she was in a loving mood before he asked her to become his forever.

HE WATCHED AS SHE DRESSED. Watched as the tiny scrap of fabric she called underwear slid up her thighs. He had second thoughts about going to the overlook. He was a breath away from taking her back to bed and proposing while she was in post-sexual bliss.

"Stop looking at me like you want to eat me." She hopped into her jeans and slid on her boots.

"I always want to eat you. I'd live on you if I thought it was possible." Mark picked up his keys and waited for her to follow. "Bring your camera."

"Where are we going?"

"Back to our place. The sunset should be beautiful." He opened the door and waited for her to exit.

She adjusted the lens and snapped a few pictures of the newly blooming crocus. "It's going to be cold." Weather in the mountains was always unpredictable.

"I'll keep you warm."

She giggled. "I bet. Don't you ever get tired?"

He gave her a punishing kiss for thinking he'd ever tire of her or the passion they shared. "Never." He opened the door and helped her inside. "I could make love to you for days and never get enough."

She buckled her seatbelt and twisted to look at him. "Tell me that in ten years."

"I'll tell you that in twenty and thirty and forty years." He closed the door and checked his pocket for the ring.

While he would have wanted to give Poppy a ring of his choosing, he understood the sentiment. Carol could not be here in person, but she'd be there each time Poppy looked at her ring.

As planned, Trig had the four-wheeler ready. He'd also put together a basket with champagne, cheese, crackers, and fruit. Mark was fairly certain Trig's wife Charlie had something to do with all the extras. Once he'd told Trig he was proposing, Mark was certain the whole town would know. Gossip spread through Aspen Cove faster than fire. Who needed the internet?

They hopped on the four-wheeler and were up to the overlook in no time.

While Mark set up the blanket and champagne and snacks, Poppy shot pictures of the most beautiful sunset. The afternoon sky was lit up with oranges, yellows, and flaming reds.

"Have you ever seen something as beautiful?"

"Yes, I have." He came up behind her and nuzzled his lips against her ear. "She's standing in front of me. Her smile is like the sunrise, her eyes like precious emeralds. Her body is like the sunset. It's perfection under my hands and my mouth."

She whirled around, shoving her camera to the side so they were chest to chest. "You realize I'm a sure thing, right?"

A chuckle turned into a full belly laugh. "So, you've told me." He pointed to the blanket. "Come sit down. I have something to discuss with you."

There was a look of concern in her eyes.

"You're not breaking up with me, are you? Tell me that wasn't the best farewell sex known to man?"

He pulled her to the blanket and pressed her shoulders until she was forced to take a seat.

"You're crazy. You know that, right?" He reached into his pocket and palmed the ring before he took it out. His heart rate picked up until it pounded so loud in his ears, he thought everyone within a square mile could hear it.

Excitement made his nerves arc as if attached to live wires. The thrill of loving Poppy mixed with the fear of her response. Was it too soon? Hell, they'd waited all their lives.

He dropped to his knees in front of her, the ring still clutched in his palm.

"Do you remember what you told me that day in your room? The day you were sick and I played board games with you for hours?" His eyes never strayed from hers. He wanted to memorize everything from this moment.

She moved her legs to the side and leaned on one hand. Her lower lip pulled between her teeth as she considered a moment twenty years ago.

"I told you that you sucked at playing Sorry."

"Yes, you did, but there was something else."

She pushed off the ground and sat up tall, her legs criss-crossing in front of her. "I told you I was going to marry you." A hint of red had risen to her cheeks.

"One of the things your father told me was that women are always right." He sat back on his heels. "Did you know your mother told your father the same thing?"

She shook her head. "No, they didn't talk about their love much. Hell, I wasn't even sure they were in love at the end."

Mark reached up and touched her cheek. "They loved each other deeply. Love is a strange beast. It twists and tangles your insides. I've been tangled over you since I was a kid."

She looked down and picked at the frayed fabric on the hem of her jeans. "I guess this isn't a breakup then." Her face lifted, and a smile sparkled from her lips to her eyes.

He leaned over and brushed her mouth with his. "How you could think I'd ever break up with you I can't imagine."

"Everything has been so strange lately. My dad hated you, and now he likes you. We were poor and now we have money. My mom..." A look of sadness fluttered past her lids. "Well, she's at peace now."

He nodded his head slowly, "She had a final request." He picked up her left hand and looked deep in her eyes. "Poppy Dawson, I've been in love with you since the beginning of time. I'm pretty sure I came out of the womb knowing you'd be born someday and be mine. There was a time when I thought it would never happen. But..." He opened his hand to show her the ring. "Your mother wanted you to have this." He placed it at the tip of her finger. "Will you be mine forever? I'll love you until the day I take my last breath."

He watched her face show a thousand emotions. She went from shock, to elation and everything in between, but no words came from her mouth.

Mark cleared his throat and shifted nervously on his knees. "This would be when you say something."

She reached for her camera without pulling her hand away. "This deserves to be memorialized." The shutter clicked several times before she looked at him and smiled. "Yes. I'll marry you." She pushed her finger toward him, sliding the ring into place. "I've been waiting for this moment all my life, but I never thought it would feel this good. It's better than sex."

He pushed forward, taking them both to the ground. "I'm going to have to up my game."

CHAPTER 26

Poppy peeked past the large canvas that hung from the gallery ceiling. It wasn't a picture she'd taken herself, but one she'd found in a box of her mother's keepsakes. Larger than life, the photo showed her mother riding a big black horse. Her wedding veil, a simple floral headband with a long strip of ribbon threaded through her mane, blowing in the wind. She was beautiful but most compelling was the look of love in her eyes. It was the same look Poppy saw each time she looked at Mark. True love came from the deepest part of a being. It seeped out of the heart and into every pore until the entire person was infused in light.

"She was stunning." Poppy looked at her father, who stood next to her dressed in his Sunday best. His black boots were buffed to a shine. His silver collar tips sparkled under the gallery lights.

"You're just as beautiful." He tucked a stray hair under her veil. "You look like your mom."

"I wish she was here." One of the reasons Poppy had placed her picture first was because she wanted to feel her mother's presence all the way down the aisle.

"She is here. She's in your heart, in mine, and in every person in this room."

When Poppy and Mark set a date, the town came together to give them a wedding to remember. Since Poppy had been taking pictures for years, Samantha, Dalton's fiancée and owner of the Guild Creative Center, thought it would be a great idea to have Poppy's first exhibit open on her wedding day.

She called the show One Hundred Lifetimes of Love. It was a look at love through the lens of a camera. Hanging on the walls were one hundred pictures she'd taken over the years. Pictures of Mark, her mother, her father, her family, the day Sahara came home with Bowie and Katie. Doc and Agatha, Bea's funeral. Samantha's concert with Dalton looking smitten. Wes and Lydia. Abby and her bees. The Williamses and their eight children. There were even pictures of Otis, Sage's three-legged dog, curled around Mike his one-eyed cat friend.

Love came in many forms. It was shared by both man and beast. There was no stopping it. No controlling it. When you found love, it wrapped around you. Twisted inside you. It was invasive, pervasive, and all-encompassing. It was heart-wrenching, heart-warming and heart-stopping. It was worth it.

As the wedding music started and her four sisters walked the aisle in front of her, Poppy stared straight ahead and into the eyes of love.

Next up is One Hundred Ways

ALSO BY KELLY COLLINS

An Aspen Cove Romance Series

One Hundred Reasons

One Hundred Heartbeats

One Hundred Wishes

One Hundred Promises

One Hundred Excuses

One Hundred Christmas Kisses

One Hundred Lifetimes

One Hundred Ways

One Hundred Goodbyes

One Hundred Secrets

One Hundred Regrets

One Hundred Choices

One Hundred Decisions

One Hundred Glances

One Hundred Lessons

One Hundred Mistakes

One Hundred Nights

One Hundred Whispers

One Hundred Reflections

One Hundred Intentions

One Hundred Chances

One Hundred Dreams

GET A FREE BOOK.

Go to www.authorkellycollins.com

ABOUT THE AUTHOR

International bestselling author of more than thirty novels, Kelly Collins writes with the intention of keeping love alive. Always a romantic, she blends real-life events with her vivid imagination to create characters and stories that lovers of contemporary romance, new adult, and romantic suspense will return to again and again.

Kelly lives in Colorado at the base of the Rocky Mountains with her husband of twenty-seven years, their two dogs, and a bird that hates her. She has three amazing children, whom she loves to pieces.

For More Information
www.authorkellycollins.com
kelly@authorkellycollins.com

Printed in Great Britain
by Amazon